Even Now

by

Sondra B. Johnson

PublishAmerica
Baltimore

© 2004 by Sondra B. Johnson.
All rights reserved. No part of this book may be reproduced, stored in a retrieval system, or transmitted in any form or by any means without the prior written permission of the publishers, except by a reviewer who may quote brief passages in a review to be printed in a newspaper, magazine, or journal.

First printing

ISBN: 1-4137-0843-9
PUBLISHED BY PUBLISHAMERICA, LLLP
www.publishamerica.com
Baltimore

Printed in the United States of America

Dedication

To my parents, Bob and Cynthia Baker,
whose talents combined to evoke the author in me.

Acknowledgment

Thank you Larry, for having challenged me to get a love story written in two weeks. It only took me fifteen years! Thank you Diane, for being such an excellent example of a good friend. Thank you Len, for encouraging me to "stretch."

Chapter 1

Margaret Ammons glanced at the glowing dial of her clock radio then pushed herself up on her pillows. It was after 11 p.m. Squinting out into the black December night she could see her husband, Jerry, getting out of the car. She watched him in the glow of the car's overhead light as he retrieved newspaper, briefcase and overcoat, locked the car, then bounded up the walk toward the house with energy Margaret never seemed to have. She slipped back down and closed her eyes, glad he was home safely, angry that once again he hadn't telephoned to tell her he'd be late. It wasn't anything new. Margaret wondered why she worried after nearly twenty years of the same.

Even when they were first married, his work seemed to consume him. But it had escalated in the past few years to the point where she and the children seldom saw him. Margaret supposed she shouldn't complain. Jerry had become very successful, made a more-than-adequate salary in addition to benefits and regular bonuses. He had moved his family into a beautiful English Tudor home in one of the best neighborhoods on the outskirts of Indianapolis, Indiana. And he was an attentive husband, if remembering to send flowers on birthdays and anniversaries was being attentive. Margaret had long suspected that the one who remembered those dates was Jerry's string of secretaries who had worked for him over the years.

She heard Jerry's key in the lock and the door push open. The dog thumped his tail against the hardwood floor and made friendly little noises in his throat to welcome his master. Margaret listened carefully to see if for once he would come upstairs and greet her before doing anything else. She knew his routine—put his overcoat and briefcase in the hall closet, set the newspaper down beside his easy chair, make a cup of instant coffee, call the office to check his messages one last time, then settle in front of the television news and read the paper. In nearly 20 years of marriage his routine hadn't changed. It was just that he got home so much later now.

Margaret knew that Jerry found it easier to come home after the children were in bed; after the usual household confusion that happens in families at the dinner hour is over. Jerry had never, even when the children were little, appreciated being bothered in the evening after work.

Now Margaret heard the distant drone of the television newscaster and she sighed, wondering if she should continue trying to sleep or turn on the light and read for awhile. An hour later she was still wondering, and trying to shake the image in her mind of Jerry working late with his beautiful new assistant, Abigail, at his side.

She finally grabbed her robe from the bottom of the bed, slid her feet into her slippers and made her way downstairs to where she found her husband dozing, newspaper across his chest. With an air of resignation, she walked across the room and turned off the television. Jerry immediately woke up.

"Oh, hi Margaret," he said sleepily, folding the paper and dropping it beside his chair. "I must have drifted off."

"Why didn't you tell me you were going to be late? Jason had a band concert... remember?" Her eyes flashing at him with hot emotion that always built up in her each time he had neglected the children.

"Oh, damn. I'm sorry," Jerry said, rubbing his eyes. "I'll apologize to him in the morning."

"You could have called. He kept watching for you."

"I said I'm sorry, damn it." Jerry pushed himself angrily out of the chair and carried his coffee cup back to the kitchen. Turning, his tone softened. "I meant to call; I planned to call as soon as we took a

EVEN NOW

break, but we kept thinking it wouldn't take much longer so we didn't break at all...what can I say?" He sounded sincere; but then, Jerry always did. Sounding convincing was what made Jerry the ad man he was. He met her eyes briefly, then looked away and walked upstairs.

Margaret made herself a cup of herbal tea and sat down in the chair Jerry had warmed. She should be jealous, but she was too tired; not just too tired tonight, but just too tired in general. This behavior had gone on for so long. If Jerry chose to have an affair with Abigail, well, Margaret didn't have the energy anymore to fight it. The love she had felt for Jerry had been gone a long time and in its place a dullness of heart.

She dropped her empty cup in the sink then went upstairs. When she got to their bedroom, Jerry was on the phone, trying at the same time to get into his pajamas. "Right," he said, pulling the pajama bottoms up and trying to tie the string and hold the phone on his shoulder with his chin. "Right," he said again, slipping on one sleeve of the shirt then adeptly changing the telephone from his left to his right ear and finishing the job. "OK, J.D., in the morning, buddy."

Jerry hung up the phone with a bang. He turned to Margaret, who stood watching him. "You're up late, aren't you?" he stated flatly. "Why didn't you just have a beer and go to sleep?"

That seemed always to be Jerry's solution: Have a beer so you can relax and sleep and not notice I'm not home, is what Margaret thought he really meant.

Though her eyes were closed, Margaret could feel Jerry glance over at her. He never liked confrontation with her; it was unsettling to him in a way she could never understand. "Look, Margaret. I said I was sorry. Can we just get past this? It's not like it's the first time I was ever late. It goes with the territory."

Margaret turned away from him and tried to settle down.

"Oh, while I'm thinking of it," Jerry said, offhandedly thumbing through the pages of Money magazine. "The office Christmas party is early this year. I hope you'll come this time. It doesn't look good when you don't show up at work-related events."

"I was sick last year," Margaret said defensively.

"Yeah, well, chances are you won't be sick this year, so plan to come."

The thought of the office Christmas party filled Margaret with dread. She hated being among all the smartly dressed, well-made-up younger women who worked with Jerry. No matter what she wore, or how expensive it was, she never felt quite right about her looks. And she had nothing in common with the employees who seemed to lead such interesting lives. Dealing with the other wives, most of whom held jobs outside the home, was just as bad. Besides, being there would once again bring Abigail to life in her mind; Abigail, who was always impeccably groomed with beautiful shoulder-length ash blonde hair that moved like silk. Abigail, who always had the right words, and was attentive to Margaret in an almost maudlin way: smart, capable and efficient. Jerry made no bones about the fact that Abigail was the best assistant he'd ever had. It stung Margaret now as she thought of the two of them working late together tonight. It wasn't just jealousy over the two of them, but of what they shared together that she could never be part of.

"I suppose Abigail was working late tonight too," Margaret felt compelled to ask.

Jerry frowned over his magazine. This was ground they'd covered before. "I don't like the inference in your voice. And no, Abigail wasn't there. Though it's none of your business. I wish you wouldn't try to make me mad at bedtime. I can't fall asleep when you do that."

Oh, right, she thought miserably. *Don't upset you and keep you from sleep; never mind me.* But she didn't say any more. Instead she turned the light on her nightstand back on and picked up a copy of Catholic Digest and tried to read one of the stories. Her family was Catholic; Jerry's was not. Over the years, Sundays had slipped by as one more day in the week. They'd done the good family thing going to church on Christmas and Easter, and whenever she went home, she went to church with her mother, but it didn't seem relevant to her or her life. If God was there, He certainly wasn't interested in individuals and their troubles. Maybe in the bigger scheme for the world, but not in her. Still she found some comfort in reading inspirational stories, so she continued to subscribe to religious publications.

"I wish you'd turn off your light," Jerry complained. Then, glancing over at her magazine, he groaned, "I don't know why you bother to read that crap." He plumped up his pillows and flopped down on them pulling the eiderdown off, leaving only a light blanket for cover.

Margaret acquiesced. She turned off the light and burrowed down under the eiderdown. The room had gotten cold; she assumed Jerry, who was always hot, had turned the thermostat down. Already Jerry seemed to be asleep. As her eyes adjusted to the glow of the nightlight he insisted in leaving on, she saw that his breathing had settled into a steady rhythm. For a moment she studied his handsome Roman features. He never seemed to age. His straight dark hair was tousled boyishly from tonight's tossing around in the pillows and wisps fell across his forehead. She resisted an urge to brush it back. Instead, she turned her back to him and nestled back down hoping to sleep.

The alarm ringing the next morning startled Margaret because she hadn't thought she'd fallen asleep. She had watched the clock pass each hour since one a.m., so she guessed she dropped off just after four, the last hour she saw go by. Now she lay listening to the bells of Overstone Abbey, which sat high on a hill just outside their little community of Overstone. In her mind, Margaret saw the monks converging from all over the grounds for their daily mass. One day she intended to have a personal retreat there, just to try to find herself again.

Jerry was already up and showering. Margaret rose slowly, pulled on her robe and slippers and woke the children. Then she shuffled downstairs to make breakfast. It was quiet in the kitchen. She put the reluctant dog outside, fed the cat, measured the coffee and poured juice. While no one else was in the kitchen, she enjoyed a cup of coffee and listened to the local news on the radio.

Jerry was the first downstairs. "I made it good with Jason," he said as he pulled his overcoat and briefcase from the hall closet. "Oh, by the way, take a look at the community section of the paper. You're in the news again." With that, he closed the door and was gone.

Before Margaret could take a look at the paper, sixteen-year-old Jason thundered downstairs followed closely by his 13-year-old sister, Susan. Susan complained that her mother had made breakfast and she was "dieting." Jason gobbled his breakfast. "Hey Mom," he said, pulling a $50 bill out of his pocket. "Look what Dad gave me this morning." He made a dash for the door.

Margaret gave a weak smile. For her son's sake, she wouldn't say anything about how angry Jerry's payoffs made her. "Aren't you driving your sister?"

"Not today, Mom. Got to pick up the guys for early practice. See ya."

"I don't want to ride with him anyway," Susan pouted, playing with her food. Susan reminded Margaret so much of her younger sister, Cathy, whom she hadn't seen in several years. Her innocent look, her expressions, even the way she held her fork.

"What's wrong?" Margaret asked. "Other than the fact that you don't want the breakfast I made you."

"Nothing." Susan bit into a piece of toast and chewed thoughtfully. "Well, we're having discussions at school that are well—you know—personal."

"Oh? Who's having these discussions?"

"In PE class. And biology class. It's the sex stuff, you know. Mom, when should people have sex?"

Margaret nearly dropped her coffee cup. This was so like Susan—open and startling. Margaret took a deep breath to compose herself. "Maybe you should give me a little more information about what you're asking."

She sat down next to the pensive, overly sensitive child.

"Well, in school they teach us in the family life courses that we should be older than we are now before we have sex with a boy, but they don't say how old and they say we need to have protection. And they act like they think we're already…you know…doing it."

Margaret searched for an answer. She'd been so against the new family life series the schools were introducing, but the dissenting side lost. That was one reason Margaret got involved in the school system and had been president of the Parent Teachers Organization at the Middle School for four years now.

"Are you asking me when I think just ANY person should have sex. Or are you asking me when you should have sex?" Margaret didn't even want to discuss this with her little girl. She was learning so much too fast. Why couldn't the schools leave innocence alone?

Susan downed the last of her juice. "Any person."

"Well, when they're married," Margaret said flatly.

"Oh, Mom. That's so old fashioned."

"OK—for just any adult person, I'd say when they love each other. And when they're ready to take the chance they might produce a child."

Susan thought about that for a moment then abruptly changed the subject. "Can we go Christmas shopping this weekend? I need some new jeans."

Margaret laughed. "I thought Christmas shopping meant finding gifts."

"Yeah, it does. I meant that. But I need jeans too."

"I'm really finding it hard to get in the mood for Christmas this year. Maybe a trip to the mall would change my attitude. Hang on a minute, I'll dress and drive you to school."

Upstairs, Margaret quickly pulled on a heavily lined silk jogging outfit, brushed her teeth and hair, hung up Jerry's wet towels, then went back downstairs to warm up the car. She wondered about Susan's comment, hoping there was not more to it than met the eye. She thought she'd wait and bring the subject up again on their shopping trip, this time after having a chance to think over what she'd say.

Once Susan was dropped off at school, Margaret drove slowly back to her empty home, a hollow feeling in the pit of her stomach. As she turned the car up her driveway, though, she was struck by how beautifully the bright winter sun sparkled on the sandstone house. As a young married couple, she and Jerry spent time planning what kind of home they would have when they could afford what they really wanted. In those days, they lived in a much-too-small Cape Cod style house. They had two boys, Brent, the oldest who was now away at college, and Jason, three years younger. They had no plans to have more than two children, but Susan was an unexpected surprise nearly four years later and their tiny little two-bedroom house seemed so much smaller. With two adults and three active children, the house was always full. They'd been able to purchase this home and Margaret thought all their problems would be over. She was sure Jerry worked as long and as much as he did in order to be able to afford a larger house and that as soon as he succeeded at that, life would be different. But it wasn't. As Margaret thought back now, it seemed the days in the Cape Cod were happy and full of life and love—all of which was missing now.

A breeze blew the stately evergreens lining the driveway in a gentle, welcoming motion, and the sunlight danced from the windows. It was so beautiful; Margaret decided to run inside and get the camera. The day was cold but Margaret was refreshed and invigorated as she walked around the house snapping far more photographs than she intended. She would have them developed and send them with a long-overdue letter to her mother.

Back inside it didn't take long to go through her usual ritual of dishes, vacuuming, laundry and general cleaning. The long day stretched before her. Bored, she snapped on the television and sat down with pen and paper to try to create a Christmas shopping list. She had no energy for it. Maybe on the weekend, when she and Susan went shopping she'd be inspired.

As late afternoon came, Margaret began to prepare for the upcoming PTO meeting, which promised, for a change, to be very interesting. As President for the fourth year in a row, she had already scheduled a speaker—a controversial school board member, which would have provided some lively speech in and of itself. But this morning she heard on the news that the Superintendent of Schools had just been fired. It suddenly dawned on her that people would use tonight's meeting to sound off. Some people would be very angry;

others glad to be rid of him. Probably the Press would be there. It occurred to Margaret then to find the newspaper Jerry had spoken about earlier. She had to rummage through the trash, but she found the local community section and turned right to it. They had run the same photograph they always did, one taken when she was first installed as President. It wasn't a bad photograph, but it was nearly four years old now.

The article was about the upcoming meeting and the scheduled speaker. Any other time she would be glad they saved space to mention the meeting; with the firing of the Superintendent, though she wished they hadn't. Margaret fished in the trash for more past issues of the paper and clipped articles that covered the controversy to refresh her memory. Then she sat back with a cup of coffee and thumbed through Robert's Rules of Order. Usually the meetings were fairly casual on parliamentary procedure, but this one might prove different.

At four o'clock, when the kids usually would be coming home, she remembered Jason had basketball practice and Susan had art club. It was dinnertime when they both came crashing through the door. Margaret sat down to eat with her ravenous son and her picky daughter, then slipped away to get dressed for the meeting.

"Susan," Margaret called up the stairs to her daughter as she put on her coat. "It's your turn to do the dishes."

There was considerable clumping of feet in the upstairs hall as Susan, long brown hair flowing around her pretty oval face, arrived at the top of the winding staircase. "No, Mom. I traded with Jason." She brushed her hair back from her eyes with a sweeping motion.

"No way," the unmistakably adolescent male voice wailed from the den.

"I did. Remember last Thursday?"

Jason began to protest further. Margaret sighed. "Do them together and stop arguing. I've got to go. I'll be back as early as I can and be sure to get your homework done. Anything you need to tell me before I go? Remember, I'll be seeing your teachers tonight!" Margaret laughed leaving that mock warning hanging in the air as she closed the door and went to the car, grateful to leave the disgruntled voices of her children behind. Once in the car, Margaret shivered. Nighttime temperatures that December had hovered around 20 degrees; she was already tired of winter and it hadn't even really begun.

Glancing in the mirror while the car warmed, she applied a little mauve lipstick to her bow-shaped lips and dabbed a bit on the cheeks, which she then massaged to blend across her high cheekbones. Her dark hair was pulled away from her face in a casual twist that she held in place with one large clip. Sometimes she considered getting her hair cut short, but after all these years, she wasn't sure she could handle the change. Her self-confidence had dropped to an all-time low since Abigail came into her husband's life. Abigail...that name had dug so deeply into her soul since the woman began working with Jerry.

Margaret took one more look in the mirror and sighed. She'd be forty shortly after the New Year. Here, in the dark under the glow of a street lamp, she looked younger than that. But she felt older.

It wasn't that her life wasn't fine. It certainly was. She had all the things she'd ever dreamed of having—a family, enough money to live well... and she had lots of activities, like the Middle School Parent Teachers Organization. She almost couldn't remember when she wasn't president. It wasn't a job most other people wanted. No glamour. But Margaret hadn't wanted glamour; she wanted input. Besides, she enjoyed the respect she got from the teachers, staff and even the students who easily recognized her now. Yes, she had to admit that being the president of the PTO gave her recognition and filled the void.

Years ago, when the children started school, Margaret approached Jerry about going to work. But he wouldn't hear of it. "I don't want my wife out working," he had said. "At least wait until they are older."

And suddenly the children were older—Susan was now in the eighth grade, Jason the tenth and Brent a sophomore at The University of Virginia. As Margaret took stock of her life, she realized she hadn't held a job since the mid 1960s. The workforce had changed; she didn't think she'd fit. She'd been away too long.

Putting her car in reverse, she backed out of her driveway. It was only four blocks to the school; if it had been better weather, she would have walked. Her thoughts turned abruptly to the meeting. She would moderate questions and answers between the school board representative and those attending the meeting, which was usually only a handful. But tonight, since the superintendent's firing, who knew what would happen. Overstone was a town known for rallying to the support of someone they cared about, and many cared about that superintendent.

At the school parking lot she pulled her full-length royal blue coat tightly around herself, grabbed her briefcase that bulged with papers, and ran up the sidewalk to the door to escape the wind. The run made her feel a little more alive as the cold air filled her lungs. She entered the school confidently.

"Have you heard?" Ginny Ashwell whispered excitedly, grabbing Margaret's arm.
"You mean about Bob Parker?"
"Yes," Ginny said, eyes wide. "Can you believe it? Why did they fire him? Do you know?"
"I only know what I've read in the papers," Margaret said, offering Ginny a copy of an article she'd clipped. "But I expect we'll know a lot more by the end of this evening." The two entered the door to the auditorium. "Oh, my God!" Margaret exclaimed.
The auditorium was filled to capacity, standing room only, as several hundred people murmured among themselves waiting for the program to begin. "This, in a town were we get three for a PTO meeting if we're lucky!" Margaret laughed nervously.
Ginny laughed nervously too and began pulling pens and a tablet from her own briefcase. She'd been secretary for the PTO as long as Margaret had been president and was responsible for recording what was to come. Usually that didn't bother her, but she seemed a little shaken now. Ginny had come to the position reluctantly, but as Margaret's best friend, she'd agreed four years ago to do it "for a

while" never realizing that "for a while" might mean this long. Ginny's daughter was the same age as Susan, and they had seen the girls from preschool field trips to preadolescent traumas. Ginny was self-assured, a no-nonsense mother, something Margaret admired but found hard to emulate. Margaret never saw things quite as black and white as Ginny did. Still, part of her confidence now in facing the possible fiery confrontation in the auditorium was knowing Ginny Ashwell was at her side.

Despite her misgivings to the contrary, the evening went well. The crowd listened politely to the speaker then a heated debate followed as people challenged him concerning the firing of Bob Parker, the beloved superintendent. Margaret handled the situation as long as was possible, but as people began getting out of their seats vying for attention, she deftly adjourned the meeting, leaving the debaters to their own devices. Though there was a throng of people at the front of the auditorium yelling at each other, there were no PTO officers and no speaker left. The principal soon convinced the crowd to take up their grievances elsewhere. The meeting had run only fifteen minutes over time.

By the time Margaret walked in the door of her house, it was nearly 10 p.m. Jerry was drinking a cup of instant coffee and watching the news, several newspapers spread out around his favorite chair. She walked into the kitchen and poured herself a glass of milk. She wandered into the TV room and looked down at her husband. "Hi," she said, flopping onto the couch and removing her shoes. Jerry grunted a response but didn't look up from the paper. Margaret and Jerry had been high school sweethearts and might have married right out of school had Jerry not joined the military. Margaret shook her head slowly. It seemed they'd been married forever. She realized with a start that she'd been a wife and mother nearly half her life.

"Going to bed?" Margaret called as she hung up her coat and put away her briefcase.

"Not yet...I just got in," Jerry said, setting down his newspaper and stretching. "Hard meeting?"

Margaret nodded. "It didn't seem hard at the time, but driving home, I began to feel a tension headache coming on."

In the old days, Jerry might have offered to come to bed and rub her neck and back to relieve the tension—but those days were long gone.

"I'll be up later," Jerry said, returning to his newspaper. "I need to unwind a bit."

Jerry's responsibilities had increased over the years of his employment but even in the ever-increasing pressure of advertising and marketing, he seemed to thrive. Rather than drain him, the "go-go-go" and the competition invigorated him. He also loved the travel and public contact. And people loved Jerry. He was intelligent. His large brown hair and eyes gave him a look of innocence mixed with sincerity that put people at ease and made them believe him. He was tall, with most of his height being in his muscular body, which he took great care to retain.

Jerry had been gone so much of their married life, Margaret sometimes felt like a single parent, having to attend school functions alone. When friends commented on Jerry's absence, Margaret said she didn't mind; and she really didn't think she did. But looking back on it made her feel very alone.

Thinking of all this as she wearily climbed the winding staircase and shuffled down the hall to their bedroom, she wondered if she had married Jerry too hastily. Quickly she shut down that line of thought, as it always led to a dead end. She walked into their large master suite. This was their dream house and she loved it. Sometimes she still was amazed when she walked into the roomy bathroom, which contained a Jacuzzi with large skylights over it or the library-sitting room just through an alcove adjoining their bedroom. Brent had been a junior in high school when they moved here. He had chosen the bedroom in the finished basement which offered him his own apartment. It worked well, especially now when he came home from college alone or with friends. Susan had taken the larger of the two other bedrooms because she had a double bed. Jason had been happy just to finally get his own room away from his older brother. Margaret smiled, remembering the constant tussles between the two boys.

She stood in the middle of the bedroom; the darkness illuminated only by the Christmas candles in each of the tall windows. Christmas. Only three weeks away and not one present purchased. Slowly she undressed, head spinning still with the evening's events, and considered a long, leisurely bubble bath. Before she could make up her mind, the telephone rang. She and Jerry answered on two different extensions.

"Peg?" It was Margaret's mother, Ann Wood, who still used her daughter's nickname.

"Mom! What's wrong?" It was unusual for Margaret's mother to telephone so late. The woman didn't mince any words.

"Dorothy Crenshaw died this morning."

"Oh, no! I am so sorry!" Dorothy Crenshaw had been Ann Wood's closest friend for years. They raised their children together.

"She had a bad heart, you know..." Ann Wood's quivering voice trailed off. Then with great feeling she added, "I guess I somehow thought she'd recover...but she didn't." Ann was quiet for a moment, then hurried on. "The funeral is Saturday...can you and Jerry come?"

"Of course!" Margaret replied and immediately knew she'd answered too hastily. "I'll talk to Jerry about it and let you know what our travel plans will be."

Margaret pressed the disconnect button on the receiver but continued to hold the phone. Memories whirled through her mind; memories of sweet Dorothy Crenshaw and her children—Wes, Jr., Elizabeth and Ron. Especially Ron. The chapter in her life that had never been properly closed.

She cradled the telephone against her chest, her mind a blur. Ron Crenshaw had been the love of her life; a man she had loved with an almost inhuman intensity, the man everyone thought she would marry. Even all these years later, she easily remembered their passion. She'd never forgotten him. In fact, on days when things were especially bad between her and Jerry, she'd fantasized that he was still single because he still loved her. It comforted her the way a fairy tale seems real while you're reading it. Ron Crenshaw. The older boy who'd lived across the street. The love affair after high school and before marriage to Jerry. The man she'd jilted. The man she'd managed to avoid for twenty years. The man she'd see Saturday if she went to his mother's funeral.

The bedroom door opened and Jerry brought her back to the present. "I can't go," he said, breaking into her thoughts.

"What?" she asked, shaking her head to shake off her emotion.

"I picked up the phone downstairs and heard your mother. I can't go. I'm supposed to be in Palm Beach.... But you should go."

"Oh, well...I don't know then..." Margaret felt her face flush. "If you won't be here to watch the children, I can't go."

"Your mother needs you; you should go."

Jerry sounded truly compassionate and Margaret suspected he was. He'd always been fond of her mother.

"My mother can watch the children, and I'll only be gone a couple of days; really just overnight. Everything will be fine here. I'll get Abigail to book your flight."

Margaret pursed her lips, but this time the mention of Abigail didn't seem so threatening. "All right," she said absently, realizing she had yet to hang up the phone.

Jerry kissed her on the forehead and went back downstairs. Margaret pulled on her flannel nightgown and snuggled into her soft, warm bed, more than ready for sleep.

But sleep wouldn't come.

Chapter 2

Nervously Margaret took her seat on the airplane. She had only been on a plane once before and that was this same route from Indianapolis to Washington Dulles Airport for her father's funeral eight years before. Now as she settled in her seat, she remembered the hissing of air, the closed in feeling and the somewhat unpleasant aroma peculiar to airplanes. She had been too upset on her previous flight to think much about the conditions on the plane, though, but now the unpleasant closeness was being fully felt. She was glad she didn't have to use airplanes too often and wondered why Jerry so loved flying. She fiddled nervously with the magazines in the pouch on the back of the seat in front of her.

As the plane taxied down the runway, she pulled her seatbelt a little tighter, watching out the window at the other planes waiting to take off as the large silver machine she was encapsulated in sped past and then with a deafening roar began climbing into the sky.

Margaret closed her eyes and leaned her head against the back of her seat, which was still in the uncomfortable straight-up position demanded for take off. Just as had happened each time she closed her eyes since her mother's phone call, she saw the face of Dorothy's son, Ron Crenshaw. It was the young Ron she saw, as he had looked back in 1963 when they unexpectedly got reacquainted. She wondered now what he would look like after twenty years...would she even recognize him? Would he recognize her? *Yes*, she thought confidently. *We'll recognize each other.*

EVEN NOW

Once she was able to let her seat recline, she drifted between waking and sleeping, letting herself conjure up that Christmas Eve when she and Ron came together again after several years of having gone in totally different directions. In her dreamlike state, she wasn't on the airplane anymore, she was back in the suburbs of Washington, DC in her childhood home...

Snow had been falling, making the small community she and her family lived in a winter wonderland. It had already accumulated several inches, and everyone in the close-knit neighborhood was outside watching the quiet beauty of the snow on the green, blue and red Christmas lights adorning houses and evergreen trees. As people began to feel the cold, Ann Wood had suggested that everyone gather in her house for an impromptu Christmas Eve celebration. Neighbors told neighbors, and soon the house was filling up. Margaret remembered her father preparing hot cocoa and coffee, and her mother setting out the dozens of Christmas cookies the family had baked and decorated. Someone brought hot cider, someone else a fruitcake. When Dorothy Crenshaw arrived with her husband Wesley, Margaret was surprised to see Ron follow them in. Tall and smiling, he greeted everyone and winked at her.

"I thought he was married and living out of state," Margaret had whispered to her mother as they carried coats to the bedroom

"His wife left him a few months ago," Ann had whispered back. "Took the baby and disappeared."

"How sad," Margaret frowned, remembering what a fun-loving person Ron had been from boyhood until she lost touch with him.

Later that evening, Margaret and Ron easily caught up on each other's lives. They were the only two young people among all the neighbors, so they found a corner where he confided the troubles of his short-lived marriage. Margaret had listened with compassion, but had not been able to shake the growing attraction she was feeling for him. It was amazing, she thought, how strongly she had been drawn to this person she'd known practically all her life. All through their teen years, Ron made no secret of the fact that he had a crush on her, but she'd never been able to think of him as anything other than one of the neighbors. He had graduated high school several years before her and gone off to college, married, and this was the first time she'd seen him since. She wondered if Ron could tell how unreasonably hard her heart was beating just sitting next to him, and she had been embarrassed by such surprisingly intense emotion on her part.

Margaret roused slightly from her semi-sleep as the plane hit turbulence. She glanced around to remind herself where she really was. All she could see out the window was clouds. The plane continued to bump and tilt, and she pulled her seatbelt tighter. "Oh, God," she whispered, but she seemed to be the only one concerned. Fearful but trying to be brave, she again closed her eyes to go back to the comforting memory of Christmas 1963.

She remembered that as she listened to Ron as she shared his pain regarding his shattered marriage, she wanted desperately to touch him. In all the years they'd known each other, they'd never touched. She hadn't ever before then wanted to touch him. But at that moment, it was all she could think of.

After it seemed he had emptied himself of all emotion, he glanced at his watch. "I have to go," he had said in his soft, smooth voice. And he took her by the hand and led her toward the living room away from the gathered crowd. There it was possible to hear the soft strains of Christmas music being played on the RCA hi fi downstairs. He smiled down into her eyes, took her gently in his arms and held her close, swaying slowly to the music. She had wanted the night to go on forever. But the music stopped and Ron had gone home.

Margaret shook herself back to the present as the stewardess touched her arm. "Lunch?" the smartly coifed woman inquired. Margaret nodded, pulled down the tray in front of her and tried to be reasonable about the feelings she was experiencing.

That Christmas of 1963 sparked off the most intense romance Margaret had ever known, exceeding any feelings she ever had before or since. They were a couple for only one short year; a most wonderful year…the only downside being that Ron never mentioned the word love. Though it was clear to everyone around them something special had happened between them, Ron never talked about commitment, either. Nineteen-year-old Margaret was devastated. So when Ron took a job 200 miles away without inviting her to join him or even indicating that one day he would, Margaret found herself alone much of the time.

Meanwhile Jerry had come home from serving in Vietnam. He and Margaret picked up where they'd left off in high school. Jerry quickly made his intentions known and before she knew it, they were married. Eloped, upsetting her mother, his mother and most of all perhaps Dorothy Crenshaw. The day after she married Jerry she knew she shouldn't have done it. She pined for Ron, and with tears pouring onto the paper, sat down and wrote him a letter to tell him what she'd done. He never responded.

The involuntary closing of her ears as the plane lost altitude brought her back to the present and she realized with a start that below was Dulles Airport; her destination.

She remembered the days when her family used to visit the airport, newly completed in 1962. Very few planes landed then. In fact, back then her mother asked a ticket agent if any planes would be landing. It was so exciting to go up on the observation deck and watch one of the new jet airplanes stream out of the sky. Only a few people were ever in the airport in those days, most of whom were sightseeing. The huge front window and the high modern-looking tower made the airport a facility for the future. These days, more than two decades later, there was so much security and so many people that children could no longer run through the wide center section of the main terminal and toss coins over the side of the wrought iron railing into the fountain and pool on the level below.

Now only passengers were allowed in these areas. It was a sad testimony to humankind, Margaret thought as she disembarked from the mobile lounge and made her way to the baggage claim area where her mother and younger sister, Cathy, greeted her.

"I'm so glad you could come," Ann Wood said, the pain of losing a good friend still haunting her expression. She hugged her daughter tightly, tears sitting precariously on the rim of her eyelids. "So Jerry and the kids couldn't come with you" she added, without too much disappointment.

"School...work," Margaret said simply, and Ann nodded.

"Who's looking after the kids?" asked Cathy, who knew Jerry's propensity for being absent from the home.

"Jerry's mother," she said, giving her sister a quick hug. "She's recuperated well from her surgery and besides, the kids don't need a lot of looking after—just someone to be there."

As the trio waited downstairs in the main terminal for the luggage to appear on the circular moving contraption, Margaret contemplated the stern Mrs. Ammons who was about as warm as an icicle, taking care of her children. The woman had always kept her emotions in check, if she even possessed any. Jerry had told stories of getting no affection as a little boy. If he wanted to sit in his mother's lap, she told him it would wrinkle her clothes; if he wanted a hug, she admonished him not to hang on her. Though he was terrified of the dark, she refused to allow him a night-light, which probably explained his desire to have one now. Always an optimist, Margaret thought that as the children were born, Mrs. Ammons would soften. She hadn't, but Jerry seemed to need to have her around. It could be difficult for the children, but they could handle it for a few days.

Each woman grabbed one of Margaret's bags off the luggage carousel and headed out to the parking lot. "How long do you plan to stay," Cathy puffed, half dragging the largest of the suitcases. "From the looks of your luggage, you're moving in!"

Margaret laughed and switched bags with her. Once they stepped outside, Margaret looked up at the sky and sniffed the air. "Expecting snow?" she asked.

"Who knows?" her mother answered. "They are always saying a chance of snow at this time of year, just so they won't be wrong."

Cathy added, "The forecast says rain, because the temperature was supposed to go up to near 50, but I don't think it made it," she added wryly as they all saw their breath hanging in front of them.

The charming old house in the suburbs of Washington, DC looked the same. The large, wrap-around porch that Margaret used to ride her tricycle on when she was little, and the giant oaks surrounding the place that had been such fun to climb. Margaret felt odd sensations of being a child again as she entered the bedroom that had been hers for nearly 18 years. She quickly unpacked, hanging up her gray wool suit, several pairs of winter slacks, blouses, sweaters, two dresses and her coat. Then she began filling the dresser drawers with socks, lingerie and stockings. *Cathy's right*, she thought, *I did bring too much.*

After changing out of her travel clothes, she went to the window and looked across the street toward the Crenshaw home. This whole business—going home, attending a friend's funeral, and seeing an old love—it was almost more than she could bear.

Chapter 3

Margaret closed the bedroom door and trotted down the stairs to the living room where her mother had a cup of coffee waiting.

Ann Wood was sixty-two years old, trim and still very attractive. She colored her naturally blond hair to cover the little bit of white that had begun to show only a few years earlier. Her makeup was discreet; her manner of dress impeccable. Unlike Cathy who was always willing to do her own thing, Margaret spent her childhood trying to be like her mother.

Margaret was aware that since arriving back at the house, her mother seemed much more calm than she sounded in her urgent telephone conversation just a couple of days earlier when she asked her to come to the funeral. Margaret expected to find her mother distraught, but nothing could be farther from the truth.

As the three women curled up in front of the glowing fire on the soft, familiar deep sofa, they talked easily and Margaret knew a sense of freedom to be herself, something she hadn't experienced in a long time. Cathy talked about her new apartment in Baltimore, Maryland, and her work at Johns Hopkins Hospital. With the exuberance of youth, Cathy brought Margaret up to date on her love life, her friends, a recent skiing trip to Colorado and anything else she could wedge into the conversation.

Ann mostly listened to the exchange between her two daughters, but she discreetly spoke of someone named Bill—a good friend who was teaching her the finer points of golf, bowling and ballroom dancing. Margaret sensed immediately that Bill was someone special; she felt a funny twinge to think of her mother having a boyfriend.

Margaret wanted to somehow express how proud she was of her ability to lead the middle school PTO to some important changes in the school, but it seemed so mundane compared to her sister's work at the hospital and her mother's extravagant social life. So she bragged about the children and their successes and she confided Jerry's new salary. But her own life, she admitted ruefully, held little excitement other than through the children's successes. "I guess that's how it is for mothers!" she concluded.

Ann Wood chided her. "It's time you got a job, or went back to school—or at least did some volunteer work."

"I do volunteer work, and I'm President of the PTO," Margaret protested, wishing her mother didn't have the knack still of putting her on the defensive.

"You've been PTO president for four years now. It's time you let someone else have that job. Your kids are going to be grown and gone before you know it, then what will you do?"

"I'll worry about that when the time comes," Margaret answered indignantly, taking a sip of her coffee and reaching for a cookie.

"Yes, and then you'll be wondering why you and Jerry have nothing in common anymore. Peg, you're stagnating!"

Cathy cast a disapproving glance in the direction of her mother. "Ignore her, Peg," she said, changing the tone of the conversation. "She just can't understand why everyone doesn't have her boundless energy."

Margaret smiled, but it hid her true feelings. Her mother was simply voicing what she herself had been thinking for some time. Jerry was growing; she was not.

"How is Wesley Crenshaw taking the death of his wife?" Margaret asked, hoping to redirect the conversation.

"Oh, you know Wesley. He keeps up a good front. He and Dorothy had been living such different lives for so long that it probably hasn't really sunk in yet that she's gone."

"I didn't know that."

"Of course you did! Remember how they never did have the same interests?"

"I guess I don't remember, but then I didn't know them like you did, Mom. How are the kids taking it...?" Margaret drew a deep breath and spoke the name that was in her heart. "How's Ron?"

"God only knows. I haven't seen him in years, and Dorothy hardly spoke of him anymore. I think she was a little disappointed in him."

"Disappointed? How so?"

Ann shrugged and poured each of them more coffee from a glass carafe, tossing aside the subject of Ron Crenshaw.

"Does Brent have a steady girlfriend now that he's in college?" Cathy asked. "I just can't believe he's so grown up. I'll bet the girls really go for him, don't they?"

Though Margaret wasn't ready for a change in subject, wanting to know everything she could find out about the past twenty years of Ron's life, she realized her mother and sister were not the place to get the information. "Hmm? Oh, Brent? Brent's on the verge of becoming engaged, I think"

"Really! Do you like her?"

"We haven't met her yet. She's from out-of-state. But Brent assures us we will like her. We'll probably meet her next summer, as she's going home for Christmas."

"Gosh, Mom" Cathy sighed, turning to tease the attractive older woman. "In a year or two, you could be a great-grandmother."

"Hush your mouth!" Ann returned good-naturedly.

The funeral was at ten the next morning. Though she hadn't gone to bed before 3 a.m., Margaret had risen before 7, showered and made herself some toast and a pot of coffee before 7:30. She sat at the dining room table reading The Washington Post newspaper and sipping her coffee when her mother, yawning widely, joined her.

"What time did you get up, for goodness sakes?"

"Oh, about 7:00."

"Couldn't you sleep?"

"I slept just fine. It was a little strange being in my old bedroom, though...looking around the room, seeing the pictures hanging on the wall that I remembered looking at so well when I was a little girl."

"You were hardly a little girl when you last slept there! You were nineteen when you last used that room."

"I know, but somehow last night all I could remember was the little girl I used to be. It was very strange. I even imagined I could hear you and Daddy talking in the living room." Margaret reached out and squeezed her mother's hand. "You and Daddy made us children feel so secure."

Ann turned away and poured herself a cup of coffee just as Cathy entered the room, dressed in an oversized robe, Scooby-doo slippers and her hair standing on end. "Can I fix breakfast for anyone?" she asked cheerfully. Both Margaret and her mother declined, so Cathy prepared herself two eggs, sliced ham, toast, juice and grapefruit. Gathering it all together, she sat down and wolfed it down.

Margaret shook her head. "How in the world does she eat so much and stay so slim? She must have your metabolism, Mom. I sure didn't get it," Margaret playfully tapped her own well-rounded hips.

"You're anything but fat, dear," Ann admonished. And it was true. Margaret was not fat, but she had shapely hips and more bosom than her mother or sister.

It was snowing lightly when they arrived at St. John's Catholic Church; the parking lot was already packed with cars. Margaret was stunned to see so many people, and her heart was in her throat as she glanced nervously around, half hoping to spot Ron, half fearing she would. All she could think of was that her last communication to him was to tell him she had married Jerry. She remember clearly the pain she had writing that letter; how she knew as she wrote that it had been wrong to run off with Jerry without first giving Ron a chance. For so many years she wished she could explain to him in person how sorry she was...she wondered if he would have cared. Suddenly she was very afraid of having to confront a twenty-year-old ghost—that chapter in her life that hadn't been properly closed.

Unable to contain her burning curiosity, she turned to her mother. "Did Ron Crenshaw ever remarry?"

Ann Wood made a grunting noise in her throat then added abruptly: "No, dear." It was not possible for Margaret to read what was meant by that extremely sarcastic tone, but she knew well enough that her mother had nothing further to say on the subject.

The three of them made their way into the church together and an usher led them up the side aisle of the very large building nearly to the front where a handsome older gentleman awaited them. Ann and Cathy genuflected and crossed themselves, then sat down on either side of the stranger. "Margaret," Ann whispered. "This is my good friend, Bill."

Margaret shook his hand and was grateful that her mother hadn't noticed that she hadn't also acknowledged the cross before sitting. It had been so long, and Margaret didn't want to be hypocritical. She glanced over the very tightly packed nave and her eyes were drawn to the large, stain-glassed windows inlaid with the Stations of the Cross. It was a beautiful sight, the morning sun streaming through the multi-colored glass.

She studied the backs of the heads of several men who sat near the front of the church, any of whom could have been Ron. Would he have changed so much that she wouldn't be able to recognize him?

Margaret redirected her thoughts to Dorothy Crenshaw as the usher handed her a leaflet about the woman's very full life, including information about her four children and twelve grandchildren. Dorothy had been a second mother to Margaret during her growing up years, someone she could go to when she didn't feel comfortable talking with her own mother. It was clear from the biography written up in the leaflet that she hadn't been the only child who found a sympathetic ear in the motherly woman. It was so sad that she was gone: sad for everyone who knew her. Margaret pulled out a tissue as tears burned her eyes. Her mother turned and smiled, nodding with understanding.

As the organ played beautiful old hymns, Margaret noticed the side door opening and the immediate family being led slowly to the front of the church. Margaret nervously surveyed the group of adults and children who followed Wesley Crenshaw, the bereaved husband, to their respective pews. Tall and composed, Wesley acknowledged with a nod those he passed on the way in. From her position at the other side of the church, Margaret could see each family member's face as he or she turned to come across the front of the church then take a seat.

She tried to guess who some of them were. Some she had known when they were children and now they were adults with children of their own. Who were they all, this family that had come within a hair's breadth of becoming her own? But for one impulsive moment twenty years earlier, she would have been sitting with them now.

Then suddenly her heart stood still. Ron, handkerchief covering most of his face, entered and sat down alone in a pew immediately behind the rest of the family. He sat totally alone. She watched his broad shoulders quake as he sobbed during the entire service, looking neither right nor left, but straight ahead, hanging on every word said. Though Margaret tried to focus on the service, she could not. Her instinct was to rush to his side and comfort him. She could only embrace Ron with her eyes and long to help ease his pain.

When the service was over, Ron left quickly with the other family members. By the time the congregation had moved outside the church, not one family member was in sight.

Ann Wood shook hands with a few old friends and acquaintances that she hadn't seen for some time, and talked animatedly with those neighbors she saw regularly. Some greeted Margaret, but she was so far away mentally that she hardly responded. As the church cleared, Bill touched Ann's elbow and directed the three women outside onto the sidewalk.

"Let's ride to the grave site in my car," Cathy directed. "I can bring Bill back here after it's over. That way there will be one less car at the cemetery. Wait right here and I'll bring the car up."

Nodding, Ann, Margaret and Bill stepped slightly off the sidewalk to let people, who were now in a hurry to leave, go past. Limousines with dark, tinted windows were lined up just down the street to the left of Margaret. With a wave of self-consciousness it occurred to her that Ron was very probably in one of them, perhaps able to see her through the darkened windows.

You're an adult, Margaret reminded herself, trying to calm down. *If you see Ron face-to-face, you will smile and be friendly. No matter what.* She mentally practiced some phrases she would say about being sorry for his mother's death...or passing or whatever was the correct thing to say.

And then there he was, stepping smartly out of the nearest limousine and making his way in her direction, head down, at a very fast clip. She held her breath, reminding herself that she was going to smile and be composed should he look up at her. A shiver shook her body.

In one giant step, Ron Crenshaw was standing on the sidewalk directly in front of her. He looked into her eyes and clutched her to him all in one sweeping motion, knocking the breath out of her and clinging tightly, his lips close to her ear as he whispered over and over again, "Thank you for coming, thank you for coming." His voice was choked with emotion; his heart pounded against hers. His arms holding her tightly were so familiar. Twenty years dissolved in that one unexpected moment.

She could not breathe. She was vaguely aware of people milling near them, but with each passing moment she forgot there was anyone else in the world but Ron and herself. He did not loosen his grasp, and she did not want him to.

Chapter 4

There were no words. As if willing time to stand still, neither of them moved, both holding each other tightly, Margaret's cheek against the oddly familiar bristle of his short, neatly trimmed beard. She could feel his heart beating; no doubt he also felt hers. She thought he might be crying. She marveled at how wonderfully she still fit in his arms. Even how he smelled was familiar, a bittersweet remembrance; a stepping back in time. It was, in those moments, as if no years had passed at all; as if they would just turn from the present and walk away together into some place they were supposed to have been all along.

Margaret felt him move slightly as if he were going to let her go; but as she relaxed her hold on him, he pulled her closer. She became aware of people, including her mother, standing near, probably aghast, but it hardly mattered. She did not want this moment to end. Apparently, neither did Ron. She could not believe that after all these years he could possibly still care about her this way, especially after what she did to him.

She pressed her cheek closer to his, closing her eyes tightly, hoping to shut out the reality that was creeping in. He took a deep breath, then moving slightly back, he put his hands on her shoulders and smiled deeply into her eyes. She was still too stunned to speak; all she could do was smile back as if she understood what was happening; as if she knew what his very kind eyes were saying; as if there was something between them....

A sudden commotion got her attention as Ron's father, Wesley Crenshaw, grabbed her by the arm, pulling her out of Ron's grasp.

"Well, look who's here!" He hugged her warmly and kissed her forehead. "It's so good to see you." Wesley looked from Margaret to her mother. "You will come by the house, won't you?" He squeezed Ann's shoulders warmly. "We want to catch up on what Margaret's been doing, don't we Ron?" With that, he took his son's arm and led him back to the waiting limousine.

"Come on!" Cathy shouted from the car window, pulling as close to the sidewalk as possible, traffic lining up behind her. "Hurry. Get in. I'm holding up traffic." Bill helped Ann into the front seat then squeezed in beside her. Margaret got into the back seat alone. She found it difficult to breath normally, and she didn't notice that her arms were clasped across her own chest, her fingers clutching the sleeves of her wood suit jacket as if she were still holding Ron. The whole thing was surreal. She felt as if she had drifted into another world. Her mind was aware of conversation and people around her, but she was not really there. She had been transported to somewhere else, locked in time. Instinctively she lifted her fingers to her nose, the fragrance of Ron Crenshaw bringing him back into her arms.

If only she could escape the world right now and live forever in this moment, she was sure she would be entirely happy.

"It certainly looked like Ron was glad to see you," Cathy teased her older sister. "Is there something about that man you haven't told me?" She glanced with amusement in the rear-view mirror, expecting a sarcastic response, but there was none. And for a few moments there was an awkward silence. Margaret didn't want to speak, as if speaking would break the spell.

Ann responded for her. "It's natural at a time like this to be overcome with emotion. I'm sure Ron was glad to see her; Margaret knew the Crenshaw's very well, just as we all did."

Cathy clearly was not going to be stopped. She continued her teasing. "Don't I remember you dated him once? Got anything you want to share with me, Sis?"

Margaret met her sister's eyes in the rear view mirror and managed a silly face.

Ann shifted uncomfortably and once again Margaret thought there was something her mother wanted to add to what she'd said, but was withholding information. Bill filled the silence then. "At a time like this, it's always good to have special friends around," he observed kindly.

Cathy was not ready to let the matter rest, however. "Wonder how come a good-looking guy like Ron never remarried?"

"Who knows," Ann shrugged.

But Margaret thought she knew why he'd not remarried, and the reason she imagined filled her with guilt. Ron had loved her for years when they were teenagers. She'd made no pretense of interest. Then later he fell in love and married, and his wife also rejected him. And then, after telling him over and over how much she loved him, Margaret jabbed the knife in and turned it by running off with Jerry.

Margaret remembered that long-ago conversation when they got together on Christmas Eve 1963. Ron told her his wife had all but convinced him that he was a failure as a man. But Margaret had done worse: after convincing him it was all right to trust a woman again, she rejected him, probably leaving him thinking every aspersion his wife had thrown at him was true.

Throughout their courtship, just the memory of his touch throughout the day was enough to keep her in turmoil. Never before had she had such intense feelings for anyone. When they would finally come together, the completeness of it all was nothing short of ecstasy. Though their affair went against everything she'd been taught, even now, as she remembered being with him, it seemed right. It seemed right still. In the midst of this magical fantasy, it seemed somehow as if Jerry should understand that she had to be with Ron again. Though her head tried to interrupt and tell her differently, her heart wasn't ready to listen.

"Well, when we get home, you and I are going to have to talk about this, Sis. I'd say Ron Crenshaw still has a thing for you. I want to know everything. They way he looked at you was so—so romantic! Does he know you're very married?"

Very married? Margaret heard her own voice resounding sarcastically inside her head.

"Of course he knows she married," Ann intoned, putting a temporary stop to the conversation.

With a chatty sister and the cold response from her mother, the magic spell was broken. She would store it away until she could be alone and relive the most incredible moment.

The car pulled up into the cemetery behind what seemed like hundreds of other vehicles. Dorothy Crenshaw had been well-known and well-loved. Bill and the three women got out in the cold and stood by the car, away from the graveside service that was going on about fifty yards down the hill. Snow was beginning to fall again, this time it was sticking. And the wind was gusting.

"Let's just head on back to the Crenshaw house and wait for them to get back there," Ann said, in typical take-charge fashion. "And we won't stay long at the house; just pay our respects then leave."

The Crenshaw home was alive with activity. Women from the church were setting out plates of cold cuts, tiny sandwiches and vegetable and fruit platters. Coffee was perking in a giant urn and bottles of soft drinks, alcoholic beverages and juices lined the kitchen counters. It was as if a party was in progress.

"Dorothy would have wanted it this way," Ann mused, making her way to the kitchen through hordes of people.

Margaret joined the line of people putting food on their plates. She didn't want any food, or drink, but it was something to do. She tried to put names to faces, but finally had to admit that it was unlikely after all these years that she would recognize anyone. Probably each and every one of these people had come into Dorothy Crenshaw's life in the past twenty years and considered themselves long-time friends. *Twenty years. A person doesn't have many twenty-year segments in their lives,* she mused.

Plate in hand, she wandered through the large old Victorian home, which was filled with almost as many childhood memories as her own. Making her way into the parlor, she breathed the familiar smelling air of this seldom-used, exquisitely decorated room. It was in here where she and Ron had spent many evenings together in each other's arms. She sat on the same couch they had shared and ran her hand along it. A stinging memory of that moment surfaced, when Ron and she were locked in each other's arms, she had bravely whispered to him that she loved him. It was the first time she had told a man that. He had smiled deeply into her eyes, but said nothing. There had been love in his expression, but the words had not come. Not that night; not ever. She was not sorry, though, that she had told him. For it was true. She loved him. Not the way she had loved Jerry in high school; not even the way she loved Jerry when she married him. It was a once-in-a-lifetime kind of love; deep and primal. She never expected to have that kind of love again.

Cars began pulling into the long, winding tree-lined driveway and Margaret realized that the family would soon be filing in. She had mixed emotions about seeing Ron again, not wanting the fantasy to end. She wanted, rather, to languish in the feelings he evoked when he held her, and slip away into that world. The hug at the funeral may have indeed been legitimate to comfort him; to bridge the years that had passed and the pain of his loss. Perhaps she had totally misread what happened. If so, she needed time to get past it and seeing Ron now would not help. Not if it meant polite conversation and generalities; not if it destroyed the mystery of the moment at the church.

"Hello," Ron was suddenly standing right behind her in the parlor, his voice smooth and soft as velvet.

Margaret whirled around and their eyes met. She felt shy, unable to speak or even to know what to say.

"You look fabulous," he said, his expression slightly pained.

"So do you," she said, her voice low and unfamiliar. "You haven't changed."

Ron threw back his head and laughed loudly. It made Margaret's heart leap for joy to hear him laugh. So he was happy, she thought, basically a happy person.

Wesley Crenshaw appeared, drink in hand. "Well, stranger, how've you been? We sure have missed you around here." His eyes twinkled as he glanced mischievously from Margaret to Ron. She blushed.

Soon there were so many people crowded in each of the rooms that it was almost impossible to move around in the house. Ron was popular, Margaret observed. People were drawn to him and children, probably nieces and nephews, were vying for his attention.

"I'd like to have a chance to talk to you before you go back to Indiana," Ron said, quickly pulling her aside. "But it won't be possible today. Can you get away tomorrow? Maybe for an early lunch?"

Margaret nodded, wondering how that would go over with her mother. Ron disappeared and she squeezed her way into the kitchen for a glass of something stronger than the coffee she was drinking. A tray of filled wineglasses sat on the kitchen counter, red at one end, white at the other. The warm, red liquid was just calming her when Ron appeared again and grabbed her hand. "Come on," he said enthusiastically pulling her behind him. "There's someone I want you to meet."

It was easy holding his hand; comfortable; right. Margaret glanced at her mother's next-door neighbor who was staring, her mouth all but dropping open. She just smiled as they went past.

Ron stopped in front of a well-dressed, attractive woman about Margaret's age. The woman was sitting in Wesley Crenshaw's favorite chair with a full plate in her lap looking at the television, apparently totally at home. "Alice," Ron said getting her attention. "This is Margaret Wood...well, I like to think of her as Wood, I can't remember her married name..."

"Ammons," Margaret said, oddly reluctant to speak it. She shook hands with Alice, a woman who had a business-like countenance, short, salt-and-pepper hair and an unreadable expression on her face. *This must be Ron's girlfriend*, Margaret thought, feeling unreasonable disappointment.

"Ammons, of course," Ron repeated. "Well, Wood suits you better. Margaret, this is Alice Myers. Alice, Margaret is the one I've told you so much about."

Alice raised her eyebrows. "Oh, yes. How nice to finally meet you. Ron talks about you all the time."

Margaret was stunned. He talks about her? After all this time? With every passing moment she felt more and more as if she had walked onto a stage into the middle of a play without knowing her lines. Ron was distracted by another guest."I'll leave you two to talk; be back in a minute."

Alice spoke again. "You're here from Indiana, aren't you?"

"Yes, I am. But I grew up here."

"Well, we all know that," Alice said, sipping an alcoholic beverage. "Ron was wondering if you'd come back for the funeral."

"Oh? Well...of course. His mother and I were very close."

Alice peered into Margaret's eyes. "Well, it's good you came—he really wanted to see you."

Margaret blushed. "I wanted to see him, too," Margaret was trying to make normal conversation in which was becoming an extremely abnormal situation. "I wasn't sure if I'd recognize him after all these years." She gave a nervous laugh.

"Well, no doubt he'd recognize you," Alice said emphatically. "For that matter, so would I. I've seen your picture. You haven't changed that much."

Margaret was stunned. Her mind felt like mush. Who was this not-very-friendly woman who seemed to share Ron's life? So many questions raced through her head, but none seemed appropriate.

An awkward silence turned into minutes that dragged as Margaret took a sip of her wine and pretended to be interested in the football game Alice was watching on television. She felt as if there was some secret that everyone was in on but she; as if suddenly someone would yell "Surprise, you're on Candid Camera," and the unreal would be made real. Well, she thought with a sudden rush of confidence. Whatever was happening, wherever this was leading, she intended to be a player, not a pawn. She took a deep breath and went to find Ron.

Chapter 5

Ron was talking animatedly with guests who had gathered around the amply laden table in the dining room. A small child clung to his leg. He had always gotten on so well with everyone. She wondered who the child was. She realized she had been simply standing and staring when a tall, thin man touched her arm. "Aren't you Margaret Wood?"

She smiled at the use of her maiden name. "Yes," she answered.

"I'm Anthony Barrett. I graduated a little ahead of you—in Ron's graduating class. You probably don't remember me."

"Of course, Anthony! It's nice to see you again," Margaret gushed, surprising herself with her enthusiasm. And soon there were others gathering around her, some she remembered, some she did not, who had been friends back in those days with the overly popular Crenshaw family and therefore knew Margaret—or knew of Margaret—as well. Everyone, it seemed, had some comment to make about Ron and Margaret's former relationship. A few people expressed regret that they had gone their separate ways; an attitude Margaret found strange after all these years. Coming back to her hometown and visiting Ron's childhood home was like stepping back in time. She had gone forward and to a great extent shaken off the past. What a surprise that for those who stayed behind, the past was so very real.

"Don't look so serious," Ron said, winking at her and once again slipping his hand in hers. It seemed such a natural thing to do that she forgot to be self-conscious. In fact, she glowed. She enjoyed being trapped in this time warp, back in 1963 when she belonged to Ron. Perhaps in a way she had always belonged to him.

The afternoon was wearing on and Margaret knew the time was coming when she would have to tear herself away and leave this world of make believe. She was surprised her mother hadn't already announced it was time to go, but Ann Wood had gotten caught up in a conversation with an especially talkative neighbor. Margaret found pleasure in studying Ron as he dealt adeptly with his guests, all traces of his grief seemingly vanished. Ron had always been a pleasant looking man, but with age he had become more attractive. His short but full beard was most flattering. The laughter lines around his eyes made his ruddy complexion seem merry and alive. And when he looked at her, she still felt he could see right into her soul.

Though she found him turning to catch her eye often, she could not lock eyes with him. It was too painful in the pit of her stomach; turned it inside out, and she had the disconcerting feeling he knew her every thought. To control herself and her emotions, she looked away every time his eyes caught hers. But their hands were joined, and for whatever time she had with him, she sought this connection.

Ann Wood suddenly appeared, standing in the dining room doorway where Ron, Margaret and other old school friends had gathered. "We're leaving now; are you walking back with us?" she asked in a tone that indicated she expected her to. Brought abruptly back to reality, Margaret blushed. She hated that quality about herself—at the slightest embarrassment, her cheeks became flaming red. But, as had always been his way, Ron was unflappable. "She'll be with you in just a minute, Mother," he instructed Ann, with a smile that had a hint of hostility.

Ron quickly led Margaret away from the crowd to the empty parlor, which because it was seldom used, was dark and cold, the drawn curtains letting in only a tiny bit of the winter sun. There Margaret's heart began to thud against her breast with memories of that room so clear she felt that nineteen-year-old girl again. Thoughts swirled around in her head.

Ron took her face in his hands forcing her reluctant eyes to look back at him. "Why do you keep looking away from me" he whispered, his look so intent it felt as if he were taking a spoon and scooping out her insides. She could not answer, but neither could she look away. For a long moment they stood there, searching each other, remembering, reliving, questioning. Eyes still riveted to hers, he slowly ran his hand down her arm, caught her hand in his and put it to his lips.

Then he smiled broadly and the tension was broken. "Tomorrow for lunch? We can talk then. I'll pick you up at 11:30."

On rubber legs, Margaret left the parlor. She saw Wesley Crenshaw again, this time directing activity in the kitchen. "Oh, Margaret," he said, giving her a quick hug. "Thank you for caring enough to make the long trip. I know it would have meant so much to Dorothy." Margaret smiled warmly at the man whom she loved almost as much as her own father.

"I'm so sorry..." she began.

"I know," Wesley said, cutting her short. "We're going to get you and your mother over here for dinner before you go back. Have you had a chance to talk with Ron in all this confusion today?"

"Yes, some."

"Have you covered anything important?" Wesley's face turned serious. "Or is my son just going to let the whole thing go by as if it didn't happen?"

Margaret didn't know how to respond to Wesley Crenshaw's familiar forthrightness. She stood looking at him, trying to determine what, if any, answer was required.

"You two made a mistake all those years ago, and you need to bring it to conclusion." He squeezed her arm and smiled. "Make him talk about it."

Walking out into the cold air cleared Margaret's head, but it did not settle her emotions.

* * * * * * * *

"So, Sis—coffee, tea or hot chocolate?" Cathy shuffled into the kitchen wearing an oversized robe and slippers that looked like stuffed bulldogs. Both girls had spent the afternoon in their rooms, Cathy napping, Margaret thinking. Their mother had gone out with Bill for the evening.

"Hot chocolate," Margaret answered then followed her sister into the kitchen. "But don't give me all that extra stuff."

"What extra stuff?" Cathy asked innocently.

"Six tablespoons of chocolate, tons of marshmallows and chocolate chips...I remember those days!"

"That may be an exaggeration. But I do remember it always made you sick," Cathy laughed.

"I think you enjoyed making me ill," Margaret said, playfully pushing her sister.

"Nobody said you had to drink it."

"What, and take a chance I'd hurt your feelings!" Margaret supervised the chocolate going into her hot milk then took the cup.

"Want whipped cream?" Cathy said, rummaging through the refrigerator.

"Only if it's the real thing."

"Mmm. Me too," Cathy said.

Together they made their way into the family room and sank down at either end of a large, overstuffed sofa in front of a smoldering fire. Cathy jumped up, added logs and adeptly brought the fire up and they were soon enjoying the sight of flames leaping up the chimney. The television was on, the sound muted, and Cathy got up to turn it off. "Oh, were you interested in watching something?" she asked, handing Margaret the TV section of the newspaper.

Margaret shook her head. Was Cathy kidding? Interested in television? She wasn't even in the same world.

Cathy switched off the set and sat back down, this time directly across from her older sister.

"I wish you'd tell me about Ron," she said, probing.

Margaret hesitated. "Where did that come from?" she asked.

"I've been holding it in ever since this morning. And watching you two interact at the house...well, I'm bursting with curiosity."

Margaret longed to talk over the day's events with somebody, but she was almost afraid that if she began to speak about it, to bring it out into the open, the magic would be gone. Hoping to placate her little sister, she finally spoke. "I really don't know much about him anymore. It's been twenty years since I last saw him," she emphasized the twenty, unable to believe it herself.

"How did you manage to avoid him for that long?"

Margaret looked perplexed. "I honestly don't know. It wasn't as if I never went across the street to see Dorothy. Every time I came home, I went over at least once. Saw the other children there visiting from time to time, but never Ron. Now that I look back, it seems as if he just dropped off the face of the earth. Even Mom seems strange about him, did you notice?"

Cathy nodded. "I think she's just like most folks of her generation; private things are private. Besides, she doesn't want anything to cause a problem in your marriage." Cathy glanced at the floor then back up at her sister. "She knows—well, we all know, Jerry's not the easiest guy to live with."

Margaret didn't want to talk about her marriage either, which now seemed such a farce. "Believe me, Cathy," she said choosing her words carefully. "Nothing could change the status of my marriage. But it seems more than that. It's as if Mom knows something she's not letting me in on. Of course, I expected her to be grieving and not herself, which is the main reason I agreed to come. But instead she's got a perfectly wonderful listening ear in Bill!"

Cathy laughed. "Isn't that odd; our mother, dating. And isn't Bill just cute?"

"He is," Margaret agreed. "But it doesn't seem my trip was necessary at all."

"Mom was real upset when she got word that Dorothy died. She called you immediately after hearing; she was in shock. But then, well, you know Mom. She just seemed to put it behind her."

"She's always been able to do that; and expects us to do the same."

"I can tell she's really worried about this thing with you and Ron, though," Cathy said, sipping her hot chocolate and giving Margaret a knowing look. "She doesn't seem to like him very much. Probably thinks he's out to break up your family."

"That's ridiculous."

Cathy raised her eyebrows. "Is it?"

"I've been married nearly twenty years," Margaret began, hearing the number "twenty" ring again in her ears. "I've got three children and I'm not about to jeopardize that. But I don't see why Ron and I can't continue our friendship. Why should Mom object to that?"

"Her generation," Cathy reiterated, downing the last drop of her hot drink and dipping her finger into the bottom to retrieve any remaining chocolate. "I do remember that she mentioned years ago that he got into some bad business dealings. Something like that. I once heard Mom and Mrs. Crenshaw talking about him real hush-hush kind of thing. He may have gotten into some real trouble; I don't know. Maybe bankruptcy. I heard them talking about him being a risk-taker, I think. I didn't pay too much attention. I came along too late to know any of the Crenshaw family very well. And it's for sure no one ever told me about the big romance! You must have loved him a lot," Cathy went on. "More to the point, he must have really loved you. How did Jerry ever fit into the picture?"

Margaret sipped her cocoa, not sure now much to share. "I really don't want to talk about that; not now anyway."

"Okay, okay," Cathy said, raising her hand in mock submission. "Let's change the subject—bring me up-to-date on life in Indiana."

Relieved, Margaret set her empty cup on the table and sprawled back against the sofa cushions. "Add a few years to the last time I was here and allow for the usual changes in children and you've just about got it."

"Oh, sort of like watching a soap-opera day-to-day. Lots of build up, no conclusions."

Cathy was so cute, Margaret thought with envy: and so young; still with her whole life ahead of her; still in her twenties. Good career. Much more time to develop into who she was than Margaret ever had…though Margaret knew she had only herself to blame.

She watched curiously as Cathy rummaged through her wallet and pulled out a handful of photographs.

"Brent," Cathy said, holding up two pictures, one clearly the boy's senior year picture from his high school year book, the other the young man standing before a candle-lit cake with the number "20" clearly written in the icing. "Looks like he changed a lot between these two photographs."

Margaret took the pictures from her sister's hands, feeling a swell of emotion for her first-born. She missed him very much now that he was away at college, and he so seldom came home. She smiled wistfully at the face she knew so well. He was definitely the brightest of her three children and the quietest. Jerry had been so disappointed that the boy wasn't more outgoing or athletic. It especially upset Jerry that Brent wasn't even interested in watching his father's beloved football team, the Washington Redskins. "If you can't play the damn game," Jerry had said time and again, "At least sit and watch the kind of thing real men do." Margaret cringed at the memory of Brent's large, innocent eyes gazing back at his father. A small boy, not knowing what to say, wanting to please. But Brent pursued his own course bravely, sometimes looking as if he was carrying the weight of his father's disappointment on his shoulders, but usually incredibly able to rise above it. It had been good Brent had gone out of state to college.

Margaret blinked away budding tears and looked up at her sister. "He may have grown some since you saw him. He matured a lot physically between his senior year of high school and his 20th birthday. Maybe you should visit more often…"

"Don't lay that on me, Sis. I'm just a poor working girl, you know. Not much time off and very little money." She shifted position and took a sip of her hot drink. "I can't believe Brent is really planning to get married though. He'll beat me!"

"'Planning' may not be the word. I think he's just thinking about it. I haven't even met the girl."

"Do you think he'll wait until he graduates?"

"I hope he'll wait until he's had some time out of college; maybe go to graduate school."

EVEN NOW

"What's going on with Susan? She sent me a drawing a few months ago; she's pretty good."

"Our house is covered in her artwork!" Margaret responded enthusiastically. "And her paintings are all over town as well—at the School Board and Town offices. It's part of a new program in Overstone and the surrounding communities to encourage young artists. She's even been involved in an art show and sold her first painting. I usually photograph her work, so if you'd like to see them, I could send the pictures to you."

Margaret didn't mention the fact that she took the pictures so Jerry could get a feel for the art shows he always managed to miss. As she talked about her children, she realized how used she'd grown to going to their events alone. Now, sitting in her mother's house, able to view her life from a distance, she felt resentment.

Cathy took both their mugs to refill them and brought back a plate of large, homemade sugar cookies.

"How's Jason, the jock?" Cathy laughed as she sat down again and got comfortable. "I'll bet Jerry's proud of him."

"Yes," Margaret said disdainfully. "Jerry's proud of Jason's accomplishments." She glanced out the window as she chewed her cookie and noticed that the Crenshaw lights were still on. Her heart took an unexpected leap. For a long moment she stared, remembering the startling events of the day. Her long pause did not go unnoticed by Cathy, who simply waited for her sister to turn back to face her. Reluctantly, Margaret pulled her eyes from the window, gave a quick smile to her sister and sipped her cocoa.

"So," Cathy asked. "What's the sport of the moment?"

"Hmm?" Margaret murmured.

"Sports. Jason. What's the sport this season?"

"Oh, we're just starting basketball."

"Is he good?"

Margaret smiled proudly. "Yea. He's good at them all. Soccer, basketball, baseball. Jerry wishes he'd try football, but he won't."

Cathy laughed. "Remember when Brent was about nine and Jerry made him try it?"

"How could I forget!" The experience had been painful to Margaret, and the memory of that pain was not pleasant.

"What was it he broke? His arm?"

"He dislocated his shoulder and broke his wrist in the first game," Margaret said bitterly. "Men can be such jerks."

"Ouch!" Cathy exclaimed. "It's funny how kids in the same family can turn out so different."

"Well, two parents, two families worth of genes." They both laughed. "What about you," Margaret asked. "Tell me about this boyfriend I keep hearing so much about."

"Doctor—at the hospital where I work."

"Ohhh—an older man!"

Cathy made a silly face at her sister. "I'm not that far off thirty, you know. He's only about five years older." Cathy went on bubbling so about her handsome boyfriend that Margaret felt regret for her own youth, given up too early to marriage and children. She again stared past her sister and over at the lights burning in the Crenshaw's windows.

"Don't you think so?" Cathy said, bating her sister, knowing full well Margaret wasn't listening at all.

Realizing her sister had asked a question, Margaret turned suddenly. "What?"

"Sis, I wish you'd please share with me what's going on. I see you looking over there—I'm not blind. What is it about Ron Crenshaw?"

Margaret could not contain herself any longer. She had to talk or surely burst. "Oh, Cathy, when all is said and done, there's really not that much to tell. I supposed at different times we loved each other, but our timing was always off."

"What does that mean? I mean, I know what it means, but you knew each other for eons. Ever since you were little kids. What was wrong with the timing?"

"Well, I wasn't thinking really about when we were kids. I think he had a crush on me then. We had one date, when I was about sixteen. Mom made me go to Ron's college dance. I did it because our families had been friends so long. But I had been dating Jerry and Ron was almost like a brother. Then I went and spent that year after high school with Aunt Marge in California, remember? And he married Elaine Smithers who I had gone to school with. Except for that one day, I didn't see him for several years. We began dating after Elaine had left him, but he was hurt too much to become serious. I married Jerry and that was it."

"Didn't he have a child?"

Margaret nodded. "Elaine took the child and for a long time no one knew where they were. I don't know any more than that."

Cathy pondered her sister's words for a moment. "So you gave up and married Jerry."

"How did you get that out of what I told you?"

"You said he couldn't get serious. It seems pretty clear to me. How long did you give him?"

Margaret looked down at the floor and sighed. "Not very long, I'm afraid. I was young and in a hurry to get married. And I'm just now remembering something I hadn't thought of in years. It was kind of strange, but I had a conversation with his mother one time after Ron had taken a job a couple of hundred miles from here. Wes Crenshaw came into the kitchen where Dorothy and I were washing dishes together and he jokingly called me 'Mrs. Crenshaw,' which he did often. Everybody, including our mother, thought Ron and I would eventually marry. But after Wes left the room, Dorothy started saying she didn't think Ron would ever marry again. I was crushed, and wondered what she knew that I didn't. Though Ron never said anything about marrying me, like everyone else, I too felt that was the direction our relationship was taking. But that night, after leaving their home, I thought back over the months we'd been dating and realized I could have been making more of the relationship than was there. He never said he loved me; and I loved him so much I thought I was probably looking at every little thing he did as evidence he did, when perhaps he didn't. It wasn't long after that that I decided to go ahead and marry Jerry. I just concluded Ron didn't love me and never would."

"I think you concluded wrong," Cathy said seriously. "I think the guy never got over you. Today he couldn't keep his eyes off you."

Margaret felt uncomfortable. She'd opened up more than she intended. "I think you're being a little dramatic. He was probably wondering how I could have aged so much."

"Oh, really, Sis. You look at least ten years younger than you are. No, he was looking at you with love in his eyes."

"Emotion, perhaps," Margaret said, shifting uncomfortably. "Remember, he just lost his mother."

"He never remarried, has he?"

"I don't know. I really don't know anything about the past twenty years of his life. And that's a long time."

"Well, unless I miss my guess, he's still in love with you, no matter what else has transpired in the past twenty years." Cathy screwed up her nose and squealed. "Oh, this is so romantic! I can't stand it... and I have to go home tomorrow. Gosh darn. You'd better keep me informed!"

Finally the two sisters gave in to their numerous yawns and went to their separate rooms. Margaret stood for a long time at the window just staring over at the Crenshaw house and remembering the events of the day. Reluctantly, she pulled away and slowly undressed in the darkness, with only the streetlight casting a glow through the window. She caught sight of herself in the full-length mirror on the back of the bedroom door and was startled. The woman who was reflected back at her was not the same one who had just left Overstone, Indiana.

Chapter 6

Margaret lay snuggled under the covers languishing in the fantasy world into which she had been thrust the day before, forcing herself back to those wonderful moments when she and Ron shared something so special there were no words to describe it. Each time she roused, though, she remembered she was mother and a wife …all the things she could so easily put aside to relive those tender moments yesterday. For now, she didn't want to be that person. It was far too uplifting to her soul just for now to pretend. How easy it would be, she thought, to sink into a world of pretend and never again emerge. These were thoughts encouraged by the sleepy mind; the place of escape each goes to dream. But they were thoughts that were appealing to Margaret Ammons.

"Peg," the voice was soft, tentative.

Somewhere in the recesses of her mind, Margaret heard her nickname, but she did not stir.

"Margaret!" the voice was still soft, but more insistent now. Margaret reluctantly opened her eyes and turned toward the voice, to see what she expected: her mother, the woman who had been, and still was to a great extent, such an authority figure in her life.

"Margaret, are you awake?" This time the voice sounded irritated.

"Mmmm. Just barely. What time is it?"

"It's 5:14. I'm getting ready to go to Mass and thought you'd want to go."

"Not really, Mom," Margaret said, yawning and stretching.

Ann Wood hesitated in the doorway. "Well, it's up to you, of course," she said, turning to leave. Immediately Margaret felt like a disobedient little girl.

"Wait, Mom—how long do I have to get ready?"

Ann smiled. "Thirty minutes. I'll get you some coffee."

Margaret pulled herself out from under the warmth of the eiderdown and stumbled toward the bathroom. It had been years since she got up this early on a Sunday morning. More years since she got up this early for the purpose of going to church. Quickly she showered, washed her hair, blew it dry and put on her makeup. She'd always been able to get ready in a matter of minutes, something practiced through the years because her husband, Jerry, often called at the last minute to say guests were coming to dinner, or that she was expected at some function or another. She slipped into the suit she had worn for the funeral and was immediately catapulted back into the arms of her former lover. She bit her lip to shake the dull ache in her belly, gathered her emotions and went to meet her mother.

The service was a comforting reminder of Margaret's youth. Now, in this place, in this building, seeing the Advent wreath and all the other preparations for the coming of the Christ Child, Margaret felt deep remorse that she hadn't passed her faith onto her children. As a child, Margaret had loved closeting herself in her room reading children's Bible stories so often she knew them by heart. She'd prayed every night for her family and pets and even for some of her favorite television characters. In her private world of growing up, she clung to her faith like a safety net. How had she set that so easily aside after growing up? As the priest prepared the elements for communion, Margaret was surprised to find all her childish prayers coming to mind, tumbling out one after the other. Somehow, in this holy place, it did not seem wrong to pray for birds or Lassie or even Roy Rogers.

Ron was with his father in the pew they had occupied for many years. In years gone by, the Crenshaw family and the Wood family often met for breakfast at a local pancake house after the service. It had been such a secure feeling to have the continuity of tradition. Ron turned and smiled at Margaret, mouthing "See you later." It seemed too casual for the intensity of emotion between them.

Though Margaret wanted nothing more than to get home and wait for Ron, Ann decided to take her girls out to the pancake house for breakfast. They enjoyed crepes with strawberries and whipped cream, hot coffee and good conversation. Margaret relaxed. It was good to be home.

Occasionally Margaret glanced around the restaurant to see if she recognized anyone. Her little hometown had grown considerably since she was a child; town streets were turned into major intersections; old narrow highways had become bypasses. With a twinge of nostalgia, Margaret thought about the days she walked home from high school, past the hundred-year-old hardware store where she would wander with her father, the five and dime where she spent her allowances, the drug store where she used to stop for vanilla cokes. She remembered walks to that bowling alley where she and a string of boy friends spent Saturday evenings before they could drive a car; the excitement when McDonald's opened a store near their home, and of course the old sanctuary of the church that had been central to their lives, now hardly used because of the ever-enlarging congregation. Here she sat, in the small town where once everyone knew each other, observing an unknown population. These were young families who, like Margaret's parents, were putting down roots here.

Margaret studied her mother's face as she spoke animatedly with Cathy. That face, always beautiful, had an aging softness to it now. But her skin was silky and her loose blond curls fell naturally about it. No wonder Bill had so much admiration for her. She was indeed a beautiful woman. Margaret saw now that Cathy had inherited those genes, as well as the outgoing, confident nature her mother had always projected, while she had not. Margaret had always wanted blond hair like her mother's and had, upon occasion, stripped the color out of her own dark hair, only to find it impossible to create blond out of dark brown. She'd tried frosting once, and it was a disaster, the tips lightening only to gold against an orange-red background. It had been one of the most traumatic times in her life. And it had been the moment she decided never to color again!

"The next time you come this direction, you'll have to come to my place," Cathy offered. "Just fly into Baltimore. It's often cheaper than flying into Dulles."

"I hope I can one day," Margaret said sincerely. "I just don't get away alone you know. And trying to orchestrate a vacation with the kids is next to impossible. Coordinating their schedules is a nightmare."

"You don't have to keep thinking 'kids' anymore, Sis. They're nearly grown."

Margaret sighed. "Cathy, I used to think that when children got to be teens they didn't need parents as much anymore, but in actual fact, the farther into their teens they get, the more they seem to need their mother home. If I'm not home when they walk in the door, all their frustrations—or joy—of the day gets stuffed down inside and I never hear about it. Even at 17, Jason will ask when he leaves in the morning if I'm going to be home all day. There seems to be a certain kind of security for him in that knowledge. My time will come…"

"You're such a martyr," Ann said dryly as she paid the bill.

Cathy cast her mother a disapproving glance, which the older woman ignored. "I think Margaret might be right," Cathy insisted, stuffing some bills in her mother's open purse to pay for the meal. "I see a lot of kids just hanging out and it sure seems like they don't have anyone caring where they are. I hope when I get married I can be at home with my kids."

"It's an admirable goal," Ann replied, handing the money back to her daughter. The three women pulled on their coats and gloves and headed toward the door. "But you'll find out if you do nothing other than be a stay-at-home mother, you'll become dowdy and uninteresting."

Margaret felt the stinging barb she was sure had been meant for her. Perhaps she hadn't been so successful in keeping the problems in her marriage a secret from Ann. In a way, Margaret's marriage was no different from anything else in her life. She'd never really succeeded at anything, just teetered on the edge of life, her fears and shyness holding her back. Her fulfillment had come through the children and that had been just fine. Until now.

Once back at the house, Cathy prepared to leave. "Sorry, Sis. I know I said I'd try to stay longer, but I've been called to duty tonight, and I want to get a chance to rest before my shift."

Margaret gave her sister a lingering hug as she blinked tears from her eyes. She and her mother stood on the porch and waved until Cathy was out of sight, Margaret wondering when she'd see her little sister again.

Her thoughts turned to her children. It was 9:30. Probably they would be up by now, wandering around the kitchen, getting cereal or maybe one of them would scramble some eggs. Jerry's mother might even do it, though she never had been much of a cook. Margaret wondered if Jerry were home from the Florida trip; if he'd been out the night before, perhaps with his beautiful administrative assistant. Quickly Margaret shoved thoughts of Abigail aside.

Ann Wood turned and impulsively hugged Margaret. "If anything I said offended you, I'm sorry," she said, standing back and looking deeply into Margaret's eyes. "I just so want you to have a happy life."

"I know, Mom," Margaret said, smiling weakly.

"Well, Bill will be here in a few minutes to help me deliver the church flowers to the hospital. We'll then probably take food to some of the shut-ins. It could take the better part of the day. Would you like to join us?"

"No...thanks anyway. I'm going to call home, then—ah, I think Ron is stopping by."

"Oh," Ann said, raising an eyebrow.

Margaret swallowed and tried not to look guilty in the face of her mother's obvious disapproval. There was nothing to be guilty about, she harshly reminded herself. "He asked me yesterday if we could have lunch together... to talk over old times."

"Well, to each his own," Ann said, meeting Bill at the door.

* * * * * * * *

At precisely 11:30 Ron was standing at her front door, knocking. When she opened the door, she saw not the confident host of yesterday, but a man with a boyish face and shy smile as he handed her the largest bouquet of carnations she had ever seen. There must have been a hundred, she thought. She marveled at the brilliance of all the different colors; varying shades of reds and pinks, whites and yellows, and even blue. The fragrance was as sweet as perfume.

"You like carnations?" Ron asked, grinning from ear to ear.

"I love them!" she exclaimed, opening the door wide so he could bring them inside.

"Did I ever give you flowers before?"

She shook her head.

"What a cad," he laughed. "I want you to know there's not a carnation to be had in this town anymore. You have them all!"

"I can believe that—it makes the whole house smell like spring." She led him to the kitchen where she grabbed her mother's ceramic mixing bowl, the largest container she could find, and filled it with water.

"You're good at that," Ron noted as she adeptly trimmed the stems and arranged them quickly. Even in the big bowl, they were packed tightly.

"I do a lot of gardening at home," she responded a little self-consciously.

"So do I," Ron stated. He carried the heavy bowl to the dining room table and held it while Margaret cleared mail and newspapers so he could set it down in the middle. Then he took her hand and led her out the door.

The day was cold, but Margaret did not feel the temperature at all as the two of them walked toward the car. Once behind the wheel, Ron talked easily as they drove out of the small community they'd grown up in and onto the main road. He made nervous small talk, asked her frivolous questions about her taste in books, music and movies. Alone in the car, they were like strangers on a blind date.

"When was the last time you were here?" Ron asked, eyes straight ahead watching the road.

"Eight years ago... when Dad died."

Ron glanced quickly over at her. "I'm sorry I couldn't be there," he said stiffly. "I was out of town," he added unconvincingly.

It had never occurred to Margaret that Ron might actually have attended her father's funeral, but of course he knew him quite well. Briefly she imagined encountering Ron then, eight years before, having husband Jerry and the children with her. How different it would have been. She looked over at him as he made a sharp right turn into a restaurant parking lot. She longed to reach out and touch him.

She wondered whom he belonged to, for he must belong to someone. His personality, his confidence, his strong features and trim body made it impossible for her to believe he was not at least nominally involved romantically. Like someone hitting her in the stomach, the thought crossed her mind that he might even be married. There could be many reasons a wife would not come to a funeral with her husband. The thought that Ron might have a wife plagued her during lunch while Ron talked of many things, but not of himself. Nor did he question her about her present life at all. But he was totally charming and soon she pushed to the back of her mind any questions she might have had about his involvement with someone else and determined just to enjoy their time together, whether it was just today at lunch, or longer. Today; this moment; and the moment at the funeral...that was simply a make-believe time; a fairy-tale happening that would end, she was sure, not-so-happily-ever-after. And very soon.

"Do you have to get right back, or shall I take you for a drive?" Ron asked as the check came.

Margaret looked at her watch. There was plenty of time. Ron headed northwest toward the Blue Ridge Mountains.

"My dad used to drive us out here," Margaret commented nostalgically.

"I remember," Ron said. "Sundays after church. I was always disappointed because on those days you wouldn't be meeting us for breakfast after Mass. I live just a couple of hours from here," he said, changing the subject. "It's an incredibly beautiful area."

Soon they were winding down country roads where Black Angus cattle stood in barren fields eating the insides out of large round bales of hay. Giant old trees, thick branches reaching far up and out, flanked the roads; ancient stone farmhouses popped up here and there.

Margaret remembered Wesley Crenshaw's words about getting things talked out. She watched Ron out of the corner of her eye as he drove on, apparently lost in his own thoughts. She left him there. What could there be to talk out this many years later with so much water under the bridge? It was enough, for now, just to be with him this way.

Several hours later, when Ron dropped her off at home, Margaret slipped off her shoes and slumped down into the couch, drawing her feet under her and staring straight ahead trying to make sense out of what was happening. She hadn't dared ask Ron any questions, because she didn't want to know the answers. And perhaps that's why he, also, chose not to seek information from her. It was as if they were trying to be who they were so long ago, each knowing that was really impossible.

The door opened and her mother walked in. "Before I take my shoes and coat off, are you interested in going shopping?" Ann Wood asked. "I've got a few things I need to get for Christmas yet."

"Boy, do I," Margaret answered with an enthusiasm she hadn't felt in years. She hadn't done any shopping. Shoving her feet back into her shoes she grabbed her handbag and coat. She was glad for the opportunity to go out... she was too excited to just sit. Back in Overstone, Indiana, she had been trying for weeks to Christmas shop with no success. Suddenly, it seemed exactly the right thing to do.

Once at the mall Margaret's spirits rose even higher. Her heart felt light as she soaked up the season through the decorations and music. Shopping came easily. She found gifts for each of the children, for Jerry and for people in Jerry's office. She even purchased a gift for Abigail and felt none of the usual gnawing in the pit of her stomach that had become so much a part of her every time Abigail came to mind. Margaret even began to look forward to the upcoming Christmas party at Jerry's office. She'd purchase a new dress for the occasion. Life just seemed different now.

Passing a full-length mirror in the dress department of Penney's, Margaret caught her reflection and realized with a start that she looked young—attractive. Her head was high, her shoulders back. The corners of her mouth were turned up as if she were about to smile; and indeed she was, hardly able to contain the freshness of life she had just discovered. Even her hair seemed to have a new bounce and shine.

After having most of the items shipped back to Indiana, the two women took piles of packages to the car then eagerly demolished dinner at an Italian restaurant. They talked easily, more easily than they had in years. Margaret genuinely missed being around her vibrant mother; she even missed the occasional barb. It was easy for Margaret, one mother to another, to understand how Ann would be concerned about her. Especially now since Ron had appeared so suddenly and so thoroughly. It was hard to keep her mind from wandering to thoughts of Ron, but Margaret worked at it. Ignoring thoughts of Ron was something she'd have to work on now the rest of her life. She recognized well the feeling he evoked in her, even now after all this time. She was in love with him—again. And it felt so good. Right now, while visiting miles away from home, she would give it no more thought than that.

"Tell me about Bill," Margaret requested enthusiastically. "He looks wonderfully attentive to you."

Ann Wood beamed. "I really like him. I didn't think that would be possible after being married over thirty years to your father, but I do."

"How long have you known him?"

"Oh, goodness, since before your father died...we saw him on the golf course occasionally... with his wife. She died just last year. We only started what you would call dating just a couple of months ago. I was at his wife's funeral, of course, and told Bill if he needed anything to call. He did call several times, and we would go for a cup of coffee. He was lonely. Then we'd go to church together..." Her mother spoke lovingly about the new man in her life.

"Yet you never mentioned him to me when we spoke."

"Well, there's not a lot to mention. We're just good friends." Ann Wood added cream to her coffee then took a careful taste of the steaming drink.

Margaret eyed her mother suspiciously. "Just friends? That's all. No chance for more... or don't you want more?"

Ann fingered her napkin then dabbed the corners of her mouth. "I think he'd like to get married. I'm not sure I would. Not yet. It's too soon for him."

"What about Wesley Crenshaw?" Margaret winked at her mother, knowing that Ann had always found the man very attractive and the feeling seemed to be mutual. "He's single now."

Ann blushed, but she picked up on the teasing. "It may be a little soon for me to move in with him!" They both laughed.

Margaret saw an opening and took it. "What's Ron Crenshaw been doing all these years?" she asked, trying to sound nonchalant, in spite of the fact that her face began burning as soon as she mentioned his name. "You know, in all these years, it's amazing that I haven't run into him before now."

"Why should you have? He's not living in the area anymore." There was an evident change in Ann Wood's demeanor, which in the past would have caused Margaret to simply change the subject. But her desire to know more about Ron was stronger. And she felt it necessary to convince her mother that Ron coming back into her life would not alter her family situation. Margaret knew that no matter how much she might wish things could be different. She hadn't been a churchgoer for many years, but her early teachings were ingrained in her mind and heart. Leaving the children's father was out of the question. So was adultery.

"I just think it seems strange that our paths have never crossed since I married Jerry. After all, we've visited you pretty regularly."

"Except in the last eight years," Ann reminded her.

Margaret took the final sip of her wine and then stirred cream into her coffee. The last eight years of her marriage had not been pleasant; her observant mother would have picked right up on that. There was an awkward silence between them as they finished their dessert. Margaret wasn't willing still to admit what she saw as her own failure to keep Jerry interested in her. Nor was she going to verbalize her suspicions about his unfaithfulness.

While Margaret was combing her mind trying to come up with some clever thing to say to change the tone of the conversation, her mother looked intently at her daughter. "What is it you really want to know about Ron?" she asked.

Margaret was stunned at this seeming change of heart. She knew that her mother would know anything she wanted to know about Ron, as she and Dorothy Crenshaw had been best friends; they would have shared everything about their children. She took a deep breath, trying to steady her voice and find a tone that exhibited mild rather than burning curiosity. "Well, what does he do for a living?"

"He's a writer, I believe. A technical writer for a computer company."

"Didn't he used to work for the government?"

"At one time, I believe he did. For all I know, that may be what he's doing now. But I think it's computers he works with."

"Is he engaged? Does he have a girlfriend?"

Ann shifted uncomfortably in her chair. "You were with him this afternoon. Surely that would have come up!"

"No," Margaret forced a laugh. "You'd have thought we would cover things like that, but somehow we discussed the weather and the Blue Ridge Mountains."

Ann looked startled. "He took you to his place in the mountains!"

"Oh, no. We just ate at a restaurant out that way." Margaret recalled Ron's excited discussion about the old rundown Victorian house he had been restoring. But she didn't comment, instead she opened her purse and pulled out some dollar bills for the tip. "Let me buy dinner," she said, picking up the check.

Ann collected her handbag and gloves and the two women walked out into the fresh, cold night air.

It was better not to ask anymore about Ron, Margaret thought. Already too much reality was creeping in. It would be easier to hold him in her heart, feeling his love and wanting his touch; pretending that there might be some magical place in time where she could belong to him without any guilt, without any consequences.

Chapter 7

Jerry Ammons strode through the front door of his home, coat in one hand, briefcase in the other. As was his routine, he put them carefully in the closet, quickly shut the door, then wandered into the kitchen. It was 7 p.m.; he was tired and hungry. For a split second, he was surprised to see his mother sitting at the table. Snow-white hair with a jolly crinkled face that belied her stern attitude. Victoria Ammons was a little thing physically, but what she lacked in stature, she compensated for through the years by being extremely vocal. Jerry always found her intimidating and even though he had outgrown her in height by eighth grade, he had never felt any psychological advantage. It was a fact he worked hard to overcome.

Now as he stood behind her, she was intently reading the newspaper and apparently had not heard him come in. Instantly he felt like a little boy who'd done something wrong; he always felt that way around his mother. She managed to make him feel guilty even when he hadn't done anything to be guilty about.

Suddenly, without looking up from her paper, the elderly woman spoke. "You always get in this late?" She turned then and examined him over her reading glasses.

"Late?" Jerry chuckled as he opened the refrigerator door. "This is early for me. Is there any dinner?"

"Dinner? In this house? Who's ever here for dinner, I'd like to know? I've been here two days and so far as I can tell, the dog and cat are the only ones that live here."

"I guess that means the kids aren't home. Where are they?" Jerry pulled out bologna, cheese, tomatoes and bread.

"Now that's a very good question. Does Margaret ever consider having them leave a schedule? Here, let me do that." Victoria Ammons took charge of the sandwich making, snatching the mayonnaise and knife out of her son's hands. "Do you want some soup or something? How about some salad?"

Jerry shook his head. "Don't go to any trouble. This will be fine."

"Well, what do you think?"

"What do I think about what?" he asked, reaching for a napkin.

"About Margaret making the kids leave a schedule."

Jerry shrugged and pulled out a chair. "I don't think Margaret needs a schedule; seems to know where they are all the time."

"Well, she needs more to do then. Imagine having nothing better to do in your life than keep up with two teenagers. Why doesn't she get a job?"

"She could if she wanted."

"Humph," Victoria Ammons grunted as she put away the food and searched under the sink, pulling out brillo pads, sponges, dish soap and paper towels.

"What are you looking for, Mother?"

"Bleach. Can't sterilize a kitchen without bleach. Doesn't your wife keep any bleach?"

Sighing, Jerry disappeared into the laundry room and returned with a large bottle.

"She needs to keep a smaller bottle under the sink... kills all the germs; it's the only thing that really does, you know. It's a wonder those children didn't die with infection. Women these days just don't take their child-rearing responsibility seriously."

Jerry nodded, quickly washed the remainder of his sandwich down with milk and headed for his easy chair in the living room, eager to get away. He'd taken his sandwich in such large bites, he was sure it was still lodged in his esophagus.

"Where are you going?" Victoria demanded, turning and dripping the bleach-laden sponge all over herself and the floor.

"I've got a little work to finish up..."

"What!" Victoria Ammons squeezed the sponge out over the sink and straightened herself up as tall as her 5-foot body could reach. "Here I am off my sick-bed looking after your children and you're going to slip away in the night and leave me alone?"

Jerry sat back down at the table. The familiar old feeling of wishing he could run away crept over him. Except this was his house. He had to keep reminding himself of that. So while she rambled on about how difficult life was for her now in her physically weakened state, he looked at her, but he was talking silently to himself about calming down and remembering he was forty years old and capable. His father had stressed being capable. A Marine officer, Malcolm Ammons had served in World War II and Korea. He had been a stern parent who had considered discipline of the highest importance. Jerry was now proud of what he had learned under his father's tutelage—strength, ability to cope, a stick-to-it attitude that helped him get ahead in all he did. But as a child, Jerry had felt he was neither good enough nor strong enough. His father had many "games" he played with his only son to help him conquer his shortcomings. It wasn't unusual for Jerry to have to sit in a dark closet for five minutes at a time to overcome fear of the dark, or sleep alone in the damp, unfinished basement. Malcolm Ammons assured his timid boy that these things would build his character; make him a better person, able to handle whatever was thrown at him in the world. There was nothing Jerry wanted more in those days than his father's approval, but he was terrified in the dark, no matter where he was. At times, even now, Jerry could feel the terror of those places. It was terror he tucked deep inside.

For his father, Jerry had played football, and his father would critique his performance late into the night after each game. Though he hated it, Jerry sat submissively time and again listening, hoping to be good enough the next time to avoid "the talk." Perhaps it was those sessions that made him better able to withstand criticism of a number of bosses throughout the years, and to eventually rise above each one. He was a survivor... and his father played a key role in that Jerry thought. Except that as a child and during his teen years, he hated being around his father. The older Jerry got, the more he showed it; not that he was at all disrespectful, but he learned to detach, an attitude his father mistook for strength.

Jerry had one regret. The auto accident his father was involved in had not provided him a chance to say goodbye. As Jerry had reached his twenties, he had begun to feel his father had not been his enemy, that he genuinely wanted to help him get ahead in the world. Jerry wanted to thank him for that, but each time the two had been together, if Jerry even began to sound sentimental, his father verbally pushed him away. The man had been retired from the military just two months before the accident that occurred when he made a left turn on a yellow light, a typical action for a man who never had a moment to spare. It had left him in a coma. Though Jerry spent time at his father's side, he could not bring himself to say the right words. All the time he kept wanting to ask his father to confirm that he really had loved him; that those "games" were really meant for good, not for harm. Jerry prayed to be able to get that reassurance; he never got it.

Now, twenty years later, Jerry was sure Malcolm Ammons had loved him to the best of his ability. That's how he, Jerry Ammons, felt. He loved his children to the best of his ability. And when there was less work to be done, when he'd gotten to a point at work where he could take more time, he'd spend more time with them. But to make it in this world, kids had to be tough. Jerry was determined to do his best to make them that way.

He was proud that he had far more patience with his children than his father had with him. He never used a belt for punishment and certainly never would consider putting them in a dark closet or basement. He was a good father, he thought, finding it necessary to affirm himself. And his children had all the benefits money could buy.

"Are you there, Son?" Victoria Ammons asked, again peering at her son over her reading glasses. "Your eyes are glazed over." It was 9:30. He'd been listening—or rather not listening—to her ramble for nearly two hours.

"Yes, yes Mother. I'm listening."

"You are not. What was I saying? You can't answer, can you? You never could pay attention for more than two minutes. I often wondered if you had some mental problem."

"Mental problem!" Jerry stood in anger.

"Yes, like that attention deficit thing. It's a disease...some children..."

"I know what it is," he said indignantly. "And I'm not a child."

"Watch your tone of voice! I'm still your mother," Victoria spewed harshly. Then she immediately became sullen. "And here I am, prematurely out of my sick bed to watch your children while your wife goes off for some vacation; in my day women stayed where they belonged!"

Jerry muttered under his breath and went to the cupboard for some aspirin. He was used to his manipulative mother, but it didn't make it any easier to deal with. He found himself hoping Margaret would be home soon. He flipped the tab off a soft drink then threw the aspirin into the back of his throat and swallowed the drink. "I do thank you, Mother. I appreciate the fact that you're here."

"Well, I should think so," she replied.

The door opened and Susan came bounding in. "Hi, Grandmother Ammons. Hey, Dad!" She kissed her father's cheek then grabbed an apple.

"Have you had dinner?" Victoria asked sternly.

Susan stopped dead in her tracks at the commanding tone.

"Not really," she began.

"Sit down, then. I'll make you some soup."

"Oh, you don't have to..."

"Yes, I do. And where is that brother of yours?"

"He's coming; he had to drop off Julie."

Jerry frowned. "He drove you all the way home then backtracked to Julie's house?"

"Of course, Dad." Susan gave a sideways glance at her grandmother who plainly showed disapproval. "I've got some studying to do...could I start it while the soup cooks."

"Nope. Soup's done," Victoria said, placing the steaming bowl on the table with a spoon and napkin. "These microwave ovens are a joy. Eat. I'll get some cheese and crackers."

"Oh, please, no," Susan protested, but stopped seeing her grandmother's intimidating frown.

Silently, Susan began sipping the hot broth of her vegetable soup. Jerry had taken advantage of the interruption to leave the room. Now he took refuge in the bedroom and opened the briefcase he'd retrieved from the closet and began to review his day. He yawned, slipped out of his suit and tie, and lay across the bed. He heard Susan close the door of her room across the hall, and though he fought it, he fell sound asleep. Someone knocking frantically on his bedroom door jolted him awake. "What is it, what is it?" he mumbled accidentally thrusting the papers that shared his bed all over the floor.

"Jerry, Jerry!" Victoria was nearly screaming as she continued her incessant pounding.

"Yes, hmm? What is it?" Jerry sat bolt upright and worked hard to come fully awake. He threw his bedroom door open to see his mother in robe and slippers, hair tucked under the kerchief, eyes frantic.

"Jason's still not home and it's eleven thirty."

Jerry took a deep breath and tried to calm the adrenaline flow that caused his heart to triple it's beating. "Why don't you go to bed, Mother. I'll wait up. I'm sure he's fine."

"I think you ought to call his girlfriend's house."

"It's late, Mother. And besides, I don't know her number."

"Well, look it up. I insist."

Jerry held his temper. "All right. But you go to bed. You need your rest. Don't forget, you've been ill."

Victoria stood still for a moment, the retreated. "It's about time somebody here realized that. Your wife has allowed these children to be so undisciplined," she stated flatly as she shuffled down the hall to the guest bedroom.

Cursing under his breath, Jerry tapped on Susan's door and found her intently reading. "Do you always read this late?" he asked.

"When I have a test." Clearly she was surprised to see her father

EVEN NOW

at her bedroom door. For a moment Jerry stood looking around her room, somewhat surprised to see how grown up it appeared. Seemed he remembered teddy bear ballerinas dancing on her wallpaper, and much smaller furniture.

"Do you want something, Dad?" she asked after waiting for what seemed an eternity for him to say why he was standing there.

"Do you know Julie's telephone number?"

"Why?"

"What do you mean, 'why'? Please, Susan," Jerry said with exasperation. "Just give me the damn number or her last name or something."

Just then lights shining across Susan's bedroom ceiling told of Jason's arrival in the driveway. Jerry hurried downstairs and met his son at the door.

"Where in God's name have you been?" Jerry demanded of his startled son.

The tall, good-looking teen crossed the room and put down his fully-stuffed backpack. "I took Julie home."

"Where the hell does she live...Ohio?"

"Funny, Dad."

"Your grandmother's been worried sick. You've gotten this whole house in an uproar."

"Big deal. She's been in an uproar since she got here."

Jerry moved forward, hand raised, ready to strike his son. The boy pulled back and for a moment the two stared into each other's eyes. "Don't be smart with me," Jerry spat out lowering his arm.

Jason, unused to so much interaction with his father over such an event stood studying his father's face. "Hey, I'm sorry, Dad...I didn't think it was a big deal. Mom knows I usually do my homework at Julie's house if her parents are home."

"If her parents are home?"

"Yeah. Julie isn't allowed to let me in if they're not."

"Well, how the hell were we supposed to know all that?" Jerry began pacing. It was times like these he wished he still smoked cigarettes.

"I don't know. I forgot…I'm so used to just doing it. Mom never minds."

"I mind," Jerry said, more annoyed that he'd had to deal with his frantic mother than over Jason's late arrival. For a long moment the two stared at each other silently. Jerry felt the scene uncomfortably familiar; he was distressed to find his stance and tone just like his father's. He cleared his throat. "Just let me know where you're going to be, that's all I ask. Or at least let your grandmother know."

The boy shrugged. "OK Dad. How come you're home anyway?"

The remark stung Jerry. It was true that usually when he came home either the kids were in bed or Margaret just reported to him where they were and he lost himself in his own world of work. Somehow the household just ran itself. One thing Jerry did not want to be was a replica of his father. Though he'd pretended for years that his father meant well in all the things he did to him, there were things Jerry just did not want to do to his own children. Because he seldom had confrontations with the children, he told himself he was a good father. This standoff with his son was making him nervous; shaking his image, however mistaken, of his parenting.

"Listen, Jason. Your grandmother is sort of—well, nervous. She's just recovering from surgery and she gets overwrought really easily. Know what I mean? Think you could make out a schedule for this week until Mom gets back?"

Jason shrugged again and nodded, then headed down the hall.

"Goodnight, Son," Jerry said to Jason's back as the young man, without so much as a glance over his shoulder, disappeared behind his bedroom door.

Chapter 8

It was one of those perfect December evenings. The air was crisp and calm, stars twinkling in the heavens against a clear, dark sky. The impressively large home of Ralph and Charlene Simpson sat high upon a hill seasonally outlined in a profusion of colored Christmas lights. A few guests were still arriving when Jerry drove up in his sports car and pulled behind the house, avoiding the parking area assigned for guests who didn't know the Simpsons as well as he did. Jerry had made it a point to get intimate with clients like them. It was good for business.

Bounding through the kitchen, Jerry greeted Emma, the cook, and noted with approval the number of staff she had working with her tonight. She giggled as he winked and squeezed her arm on his way past. Now out of his mother-dominated house and no longer the manipulated child, Jerry was in his element.

Making his way into the large foyer, he looked around for his host and hostess. People in their best clothing and expensive jewelry were standing around in small groups, most already with drink in hand. Jerry's heart skipped a beat as he noticed beautiful Abigail in a floor-length strapless gown of crushed red velvet, which dropped softly over her gently curving hips. She was stunning, he thought. She noticed him at that moment and waved, clinging to the arm of her fiancé, Charles Pen. Jerry waved back, trying to appear as casual as possible, though Abigail had been stirring feelings in him for years.

He was startled to feel an arm grab him around the waist. It was Charlene Simpson, a woman in her late fifties whose years of heavy smoking had left a roadmap of lines all over her once-pretty face. In a throaty voice, she greeted him and touched his lips with her own. "So good to see you, darling!"

Jerry gave her a bear hug. "You still hanging out with that old man or are you free now so we can run away together," he whispered in her ear.

"Let's go anyway," Charlene laughed.

"Where is that old man you insist on hanging out with?" Jerry asked.

Charlene laughed, her ego properly boosted, and pointed to the library. Of course, Ralph was always in the library. That was where he kept his favorite Scotch, which he shared with only a special few. Jerry greeted other office people as he made his way to the library, giving each of the women the once-over, telling himself he was making them feel better about themselves. And he had to admit; he liked the admiring glances he got in return. He knew a number of them would make herself available to him in a moment, but none was as stunning or as desirable as Abigail. He'd been working on a relationship with Abigail ever since she'd come to work for him. Slowly, unobtrusively, trying to win her confidence, he began to be her friend. He also let her think her opinion on business matters was important, that her input was crucial. Jerry knew that for a woman like Abigail that was important. He made her feel he couldn't run the office without her. A man in need, was how he came across. And when he saw her tonight, he did have a need for her. He smiled across the room at her now, though she didn't see him. It felt good just to watch her. Then he slipped into the library to find his host.

In the darkened, paneled, smoke-filled room stood Ralph Simpson and two other men who were busily puffing cigars and sipping Famous Grouse. When Ralph saw Jerry, he beamed, extending his right hand to shake Jerry's and his left with an unlit cigar. "You've never tasted a smoke like this one, Jer." He handed Jerry a drink from a tray as a maid walked by. "Now you're complete! My favorite smoke, my favorite Scotch! My favorite ad man."

Since he stopped smoking years before, Jerry truly hated smoke in any form, except perhaps at a cookout, but he took the cigar and obligingly drew upon it as Ralph struck a match for him. This was what his father had trained him for, he reasoned. It wasn't exactly a military battle like his father had fought, but it was his battle—to survive in the advertising world.

Jerry had done a good job of surviving, scraping his way to the top. Now he had made it. And he didn't take it easy even though he could. That was what he felt kept him on top in a constantly changing industry. Work hard; work all the time. Go, go, go. Know the right people, mix with them regularly and often. Give them what they want. That's what brought in the clients; that's what brought in the money. That's what success was all about.

Forty years old, he thought as he looked around the room with satisfaction at the world he had created for himself and listened to the small talk. Forty years old... and set for life. Two homes—one to live in, one to vacation in. Good salary, good insurance, great stock market portfolio and an excellent retirement program that would look after him better than his salary did now. He had it all. He could retire whenever he decided to. But who wanted to retire! Not with all this—not with more to achieve. He sipped his Scotch. "Good, eh?" Ralph asked. "They say it's the favorite of Princess Diana."

Jerry nodded. "So I understand."

"You still rooting for those Redskins?" Ralph chided his friend.

"You know me, Ralph," Jerry laughed. "Once a Washington fan, always a Washington fan."

"You grew up there, didn't you?" Ralph asked rhetorically. "Oh, yes. Well, I guess you're pretty happy with Gibbs. Do you think he can take them all the way again this year?"

"Eight and two—it looks promising at least. I think he can do it!" Jerry exclaimed. Football was the one thing he could allow himself to really get excited over.

"Yeah, well, they still lost at home to the Cowboys," noted J.D. Harkins, head of the largest company Jerry's firm represented. J.D.

was an enigma to Jerry, who felt very uncomfortable around him. Regardless of Jerry's training and instincts, he had failed to really draw J.D. out or find out what made him tick. "What do you think about the next time they play—think the Redskins can beat them?"

"Sure; they've got good momentum," Jerry responded, seeing this as a sign that J.D. was warming to him.

"But they'll be playing in Dallas." The speaker this time was Michael Goodridge, a well-known stock and investment counselor who'd made millions for his clients. "Dallas is a superior team. Always has been."

Jerry shook his head. "I still think I'd bet on the Redskins," Jerry was a connoisseur of football and he saw things that led him to feel the team was going to be great this year. Though he'd lived in Indiana for many years now, his heart was with the team he loved as a child.

"Well," J.D. grumbled. "It's a hell of a note when we've got the Colts right here in Indianapolis, but you fellows are only interested in the Redskins and Cowboys."

Jerry resisted the urge to pacify him. He knew J.D. Harkins always sounded tough, but he suspected he liked a challenge. Jerry hoped he was reading the man correctly. There was just something strange about him he couldn't put his finger on.

"Come on, J.D.," Ralph said, punching the man lightly in a gesture of camaraderie. "Have another drink."

"Nope. Think I'll go look for some Colts fans." Everyone was silent as J.D. left the room.

"Are you a gambling man, Ammons?" Michael Goodridge asked.

"I buy stocks through you, don't I?" Jerry jibed at his friend.

Goodridge ignored the barb. "The Cowboys-Redskins game, December 11. I say the Redskins can't take 'em."

Jerry thought for a minute. He didn't like to make wagers with these people; it could cause hard feelings. However, Goodridge seemed anxious to bet and Jerry thought if he could keep the stakes low, it couldn't hurt. "Sure. What do you want to bet?"

"I'll make it easy. If the Cowboys lose, I'll pay a thousand dollars on the point difference. If they win, you take the same fall."

Ralph uttered a low whistle. "Hey, Jerry. Sounds like he's a serious Cowboy fan."

"Mike, the Redskins just beat the Cardinals 45-7...that'd be $38,000 if that happens again."

"That was the Cardinals. I'm talking Cowboys. Of course, you might end up on the low end. Does that scare you?"

"Well, frankly…"

"Come on, Jer. What's a little money between friends. You believe in your team or not? Or maybe you don't have much faith in that braggart quarterback Theisman," Michael said, egging Jerry on.

It was more than that. Jerry didn't want to bet that kind of money. Whether he won or lost, it would be bad for business. "How about just betting a game of golf, Mike. I don't usually put that kind of money on football. Got a kid in college you know."

Mike Goodridge nodded knowingly. "I got it, Ammons. You just don't think the Redskins will take it. I don't blame you buddy." He stood surveying Jerry, waiting to see what the man would do, judging correctly that Jerry didn't like to be challenged. "I guess I misjudged you, Ammons. I thought you had more guts than that. A thousand dollars then. Win or lose, regardless of point spread. Come on. Either you back your team or you don't."

Finally Jerry extended his hand. "Okay. A thousand dollars. And I won't sleep until December 11!"

Jerry managed then to excuse himself to mingle with the other guests who were gathered in various rooms of the house. He passed J.D. who was leaning on the living room mantle, holding high his glass inspecting the contents. He acknowledged Jerry. "Good year," he said, nodding toward the ruby-red wine he held up.

Jerry gave him a thumbs-up, but as he began to comment he saw Abigail, rosy-cheeked and tipsy, standing in the doorway to the entrance hall. In three strides he was beside her. "Where's the boyfriend," Jerry asked, helping her balance.

Abigail shrugged and giggled. "I've had too much to drink, Jerry. I think I've embarrassed him."

"Oh, for God's sake, Abigail, it's Christmas. Get roaring drunk if you want."

She laughed and finished the last bit of her gin and tonic. "I think I'll take a little walk outside," she said slipping away from Jerry and nearly falling down. Jerry scooped her up.

"Maybe you are a little tipsy," he said. "I'll go with you."

Down the hall and through the kitchen they went, Jerry holding Abigail steady with his arm around her waist. "Going to step outside for a moment," Jerry explained to Emma as he passed by. She nodded and went on with what she was doing.

Outside the cold air took them both by surprise. Jerry removed his suit coat and slipped it over Abigail's shoulders. "Maybe we shouldn't stay out here," he offered. "You might get sick or something."

She shook her head. "No, it's making me feel better. Just give me a few minutes. I feel so foolish." She leaned heavily on Jerry, breathing deeply of the cold, crisp air, her hip rising and falling gently against his. The night was quiet and still, without a sound in the elegant surroundings of the Simpson's home. Jerry was acutely aware of Abigail's inhaling and exhaling. She smelled of lavender and roses, and her breath was sweet as the perfume she wore. It became too much for him to resist. Impulsively, he leaned forward and brushed her lips with his.

"Forgive me," he said, looking deeply into her startled eyes. "You just look so beautiful tonight." For a moment Abigail's stare was blank and Jerry feared she would slap him or worse, scream. Instead, she, slipped her arms around his waist, tilted her head slightly upwards, and stepped closer to him. She continued to stare into his eyes, hers deep blue and inviting, with wet tears in the corners no doubt the result of her alcohol consumption. It made her appear vulnerable. Her youthful skin was smooth as silk; her lips full and bow-shaped. All these months he had wanted to take her in his arms and she, so professional, kept him at arms distance. He could hardly believe his luck. He wondered if she would let him make love to her. He kissed her again, gently, not wanting to frighten her away. "Let's walk," he said, clearing his throat, though walking was the last thing he wanted to do. Again she relied upon him to hold her steady. It seemed to him she was deliberately pressing her hip against his as they moved in lock step.

Despite his jacket on her shoulders, she was shivering by the time they had made their way down the brick walk toward the solarium on the other side of the house. The solarium was majestic against the dark sky, the scattering of white Christmas lights decorating trunks and branches of tropical trees kept by Charlene Simpson who enjoyed plants of all kinds. Reaching the door, Jerry fervently hoped it would be unlocked. He turned the knob and it was. The two of them were soon standing in the warm humid air among Charlene's indoor garden, a profusion of geraniums and gardenias, orange, lemon and lime trees, all in bloom.

The fragrance was heavy and piqued every sense within Jerry; it was more stimulating than any experience he could remember. He slipped his arm from around Abigail and led her to a wooden bench hidden against the brick wall of the house by tall orange trees sprinkled with white lights.

"It's warmer in here," Jerry said, stating the obvious. "I don't want you to catch cold."

He smiled at her and together they sat. She rested her head against his shoulder, her perfume all but lost in the heavy fragrance emitted by the many blossoms in the solarium. Jerry gently massaged Abigail's shoulders and back as she leaned against him. Coaching himself to go slowly, he kissed her forehead, allowing his lips to linger against the cool soft skin.

He couldn't believe she was letting him get this close; couldn't believe he was kissing her. He'd flirted with women all his life, on the dance floor, in the office, at parties…but it never went farther than that. He learned that from his father, too. His mother understood. That's what men did. But something about Abigail—and this night—was beguiling; irresistible.

He pressed his warm lips against hers. She tasted sweet. When she pulled away, it was to study him again with her probing eyes, which only served to excite him further. When his lips again found her mouth, she returned his kiss with passion.

Arms around each other, Jerry and Abigail pulled at each other in a desperate embrace. Then without warning, Abigail backed away.

"Jerry—should we be going this?" her voice was soft and she leaned back against the wall, moist lips parted slightly, eyes closed.

Jerry's heart was beating as if it would jump out of his chest. "Why shouldn't we?" he mumbled, kissing every inch of her face and neck.

"Because," she said, slipping away from him. "Because of Charles. Because you're my boss. Because you're married." She spoke that last phrase as though just remembering that fact.

Jerry pulled back. She sure could think clearly for a drunk woman, he thought angrily. He knew anger wouldn't help matters, so taking a moment to compose himself, he placed his hands on her bare shoulders and looked her squarely in the eye. "Abigail, none of those reasons means anything if you and I want to be together. Life's too short not to take advantage of every opportunity to be happy." He sounded as sincere as he could, making every effort to mask the animal desire within. "You do like me, don't you? I like you so much..." Jerry adopted a worried look.

She looked uncertain, but did not pull away from his grasp. Taking a chance, he brushed her lips with his. "I think you're wonderful," he breathed.

"Yes, Jerry, I do like you...a lot."

It was all the opening he needed. With his lips firmly against hers, he wrapped her in his arms and slowly leaned over her, slipping her down onto the hard wooden bench. She yielded easily to his touch; he felt as nervous as a schoolboy.

"Abigail? Abigail, are you in there?" Charles Pen had gotten concerned when Abigail didn't return and had gone looking. J.D. Harkins was with him.

Jerry and Abigail froze hoping they could not be seen amidst the large potted citrus trees.

"I hope to God she didn't get lost wandering out into the cold,"

Charles muttered, trying to make up his mind whether to enter the greenhouse or not.

"Was she that drunk?" asked J.D., peering around the large glass room.

"The woman gets drunk on one glass of wine," Charles said with disgust. He called plaintively one more time. "Well, if she was here, she'd hear me. And I'm more worried about her falling down somewhere outside and freezing to death."

"Maybe she's just in the bathroom," J.D. offered. "I'll have one of the women check." Together the men disappeared, closing the door behind them.

Chapter 9

"Calling home?" Ann Wood asked, appearing in the living room in her robe and slippers.

"I was," Margaret said, depositing the receiver in its cradle. "Nobody's there but Jerry's mother...and I woke her up. That made her happy," she commented sarcastically. She wished now she hadn't called; she would worry about the children.

"Your face tells me you're getting homesick," Ann observed. She kissed her daughter on the forehead. "I'm glad. I was beginning to think you didn't miss your family!"

Margaret stared at her mother, many retorts sounding in her head, but none seemed necessary. Of course she missed her family. Apparently, though, they didn't miss her very much. She was beginning to get the picture others saw—a mother who couldn't let go. She leaned back in the chair and sighed.

"Are you thinking about leaving early?" Ann asked, as if her earlier comment meant absolutely nothing.

"I really don't want the hassle of changing my reservations, and there's really no reason to," Margaret observed, pulling off her shoes.

"I'm going to get a glass of water; can I get you anything?" Ann disappeared into the kitchen, then gave a shout. Margaret rushed in.

"What happened!" she said, quickly observing that her mother didn't seem to be damaged in any way.

"I just looked at the calendar and discovered Bill and I are supposed to go on an overnight ski trip tomorrow night with another couple. We planned it back in the fall. I'll bet Bill has forgotten too. Well, we'll just have to cancel it."

"No, Mom. Not on my account."

"Well, why don't you come with us then. I'm sure it will be no problem, but I'll mention it to Bill and the others."

"That's nice of you, Mom. But three things I dislike very much are heights, cold and speed—and I think skiing involves all three. You go and don't worry about me. It's only overnight."

Ann went on about leaving Margaret alone while she was visiting, and Margaret assured her it would be all right.

Whether Ann was convinced or not, Margaret wasn't sure, but she seemed to relent for the time being. The two women soon went their separate ways to their respective bedrooms.

Margaret stood surveying the room she remembered so well during her years of growing up there. So much had stayed the same; almost as if time had stood still. The hand-painted dresser, bedside table, bookshelf, all built by her father and painted with a floral design by her mother so many years before. They did so many things together. The stereo she was given for her fourteenth birthday still sat atop the bookshelf, her 45s still packed in the pink plastic poodle case. What memories! How many conversations—deadly serious—her friends and she had held there in that room while that stereo played, learning about love from the music of Elvis Presley, Ricky Nelson, the Everly Brothers. "Just call my name," she could almost hear Elvis singing, "and I'll be right by your side." Her lips turned up at the corners as she pictured herself softly calling Elvis's name all those years ago, just in case he might magically appear in her room if she did.

As she sat there thinking of those days gone by, she was aware of another feeling left over from those days: embarrassment and feelings of not fitting in because she was so tall, so skinny. She remembered how even in the hot humid Washington, D.C. summers, she would wear pedal pushers instead of shorts and long sleeves to hide bony knees and elbows, especially if she thought Ron and his friends were going to be around. It wasn't that she had a crush on him then, it was just that she was so self-conscious. Thinking of those days, she wished she'd had more confidence just to be herself. Still, most of her memories of childhood were comforting. It was a simple time. There was always a new adventure ahead; always tomorrow. She'd been about thirty when she'd become philosophical about being tall. She'd wasted so much time wishing to be the "perfect" height, which was, of course, just shorter than any boy she might have been dreaming about.

Chuckling, she thought of Jason and how her long legs had probably contributed to the height he seemed to be attaining, which helped him be the athlete he was. She wondered again where her children were and if she should call again. She decided she would not. She didn't want to wake Mrs. Ammons. And if anything had gone wrong, they would contact her.

Margaret got up from her warm, comfortable chair and went to the front window which faced the street. In the winter she was able to see as far as the Crenshaw's house. Now she noticed the white winter beauty of the creek that separated their streets, winding along snowy banks under the bright moon; the blackness of the barren trees against a clear night sky. She stared at the Crenshaw house and realized for the first time that she didn't even know which bedroom had been Ron's. Now there were lights in two upstairs rooms in their house, but there was no way to know which Ron was using.

Back in the old days, while Margaret's own parents had been part of the country club set, the Crenshaws were campers and hunters. The boys and their father hunted deer and bear in the wooded areas west of the county and by the time each boy became sixteen, he already had a formidable gun collection. Their family room overflowed with testimony to their skill in archery and marksmanship. Each year in the fall, even after the boys had grown and left home, they went hunting with their father. It was a tradition. Margaret wished Jerry had some time to form bonds with their children as Wesley Crenshaw had with his. A bittersweet pain filled her chest.

Margaret turned out the lights, but pulled the chair closer to the window and sat rocking and watching the Crenshaw house. The surrounding darkness was comforting, enveloping her in a world she had always sought as a child; a world in which to pretend she was anything and anywhere she wanted to be. The more she stared at the house, the more she wanted to talk to Ron. What was this strange relationship they shared? Hesitantly she reached for the phone, took the receiver off the hook and dialed. It was late; she worried about waking Wesley Crenshaw. She would, she determined weakly, hang up if Ron didn't answer on two rings.

Ron answered almost before the first ring was complete. "Margaret?" his voice sounded hopeful. But how could he have known...

"Yes," she whispered. Then there was silence. What should she say; she felt odd about having called.

"I'm so glad you called. I was afraid I wouldn't get to talk to you before you left." Ron's voice was so sincere.

"Oh, I'm not leaving for a few days yet," Margaret paused, unsure of what to say. "Well, how is your dad doing?" Of all the things on her mind at that moment, it was the only question Margaret would allow herself to ask.

"Pretty well, I think. You know Dad. Ever the optimist. I'm glad he has plenty of friends around to look after him when we've all gone back home. Of course, I'm not far away."

"And you. How are you handling everything?"

Ron hesitated. "It's especially hard on me, Margaret. There's so much I didn't say to Mom... about me, about my life," his voice trailed off. "But," he said suddenly brightening as if wanting to make light of what he'd said. "I loved her. She knew that. And she loved me, I'm sure... no matter what."

"Of course she loved you," Margaret shot back, surprised he would even question it. Then she remembered what Cathy had said about there being some nebulous secret surrounding Ron. There was a minute or so of silence.

"You're thinking," he whispered. "That could be dangerous."

She smiled. "I hope not..."

"Margaret, I wish we could... I think that... well, I hope we can spend some time together again before you leave."

"I hope so too."

"I've changed a lot," Ron began. "Some things have changed, that is."

Margaret assured him she had also changed a lot. The two talked long into the night, again avoiding specifics about her life or his, but reminiscing or projecting or philosophizing about life in general. It was enough for her just to hear his voice. Nagging questions that tried to surface from the back of her mind were shoved down deep; buried in that place called "denial."

The more he talked, the more Margaret noticed his aversion to getting into anything really personal. However, she was struck by how alike they were. Almost more like herself than she was, she thought incredulously. And he was far more sensitive than she had realized. Or perhaps he'd become more so with time. In her dreams over the past twenty years, those times when she was so lonely for love, she would think of him and imagine him being that sensitive—able to know her mood or detect what was on her mind—that had been her fantasy. It was almost too much that he had intruded and made that fantasy reality. Here he was, on the other end of the phone having the kind of conversation they might have had in one of her dreams. It became hard to separate the make-believe from the real.

As the night wore on, their reluctance to close the conversation was clear, punctuated by long periods of silence during which she simply cradled the phone against her ear and listened to him breath.

"I need to see you tomorrow," Ron said softly, breaking one of the long silences.

Margaret swallowed hard. How she needed to see him too. Losing him from her life had created a sadness within her that had remained well hidden through the years; a sadness that had manifested itself in long periods of withdrawal from her family. Of course, Jerry never noticed, but she felt pangs of guilt from time to time that she was neglecting the children during those periods. Over time, she learned to be restrained; to relegate certain feelings to a deep, remote place. That was where the ghost called Ron lived for twenty years. "Margaret—do you have any idea how important you are to my life?

"I know I was important—years ago."

"You still are. I can't explain it, Margaret. But it's true." Though his voice was close to inaudible, it nearly drew her physically through the telephone and into his arms. "It snowed the last Christmas we were together," he went on. "Do you remember?"

As if she could forget. She laughed lightly. "More snow than I'd ever seen in my life. It was beautiful."

"You were beautiful. Are beautiful. And that was a very special time; a special year."

"For me, yes," Margaret said slowly, remembering how non-committal Ron had been.

"I was hurting; my wife and child were gone. I felt dead. I couldn't work; couldn't sleep; couldn't talk or share my pain. Then there you were, looking at me with such love in your eyes. You listened to me for hours that night as I poured everything out and you didn't criticize or make suggestions; you just let me talk. And then you danced with me, remember? And when I slipped my arms around you and drew you close, it was as though my heart started up again. My blood began to flow, my brain worked again. You saved my life, Margaret." His voice cracked.

"Oh, Ron—no..." Margaret did not want him to go on, because she knew the end of that story. It ended with her letter to him telling him she had married Jerry. "You were strong. You didn't need me."

"I think I did, Margaret. You literally loved me back to life," Ron hesitated. "You did love me, didn't you?"

How could he ever have doubted it, she wondered incredulously. It was a stinging question. Margaret had loved Ron intensely. And she had said those words to him over and over, waiting, praying that he would say them to her. He never did. Now he was asking her to confirm those feelings she had so bravely expressed to him—twenty years later. Why? She was so filled with confusion she couldn't speak.

She remembered her feelings all those years ago. Yes, she'd loved him with all her heart and soul. If he didn't know it, he was the only one who didn't. She felt a surge of strength course through her in this bizarre moment. She'd had enough experience in life to know that there are opportunities that are fleeting; you either grab hold of them or they are gone forever. She took a deep breath.

"Yes, Ron," she sighed. "I did love you."

"And I loved you. Margaret, I still do."

Margaret blinked back the tears that burned her eyes. The clock downstairs in the living room chimed two o'clock. They'd been on the telephone more than four hours. Four hours, it had taken Ron, only four hours, to admit what she'd longed to hear twenty years before; to admit what would have been a life-changing moment for both of them. For despite Ron's mother's warning that he'd never marry again, Margaret would have waited for him to put his pain behind him if only he'd admitted loving her.

"Margaret—are you still there?" Ron's soft voice was plaintive. "You're angry, aren't you?"

"No—no, Ron."

"Yes you are. And you have every right to be. I changed the course of our lives by my stubbornness."

He changed the course? Margaret was incredulous. She was the one who so impulsively ran off and got married. She was the one who was impatient with a man who'd had more than one difficult blow in his young life. And he had been young. So had she.

"Margaret, before you go back to Indiana, I want to take you out and show you my house in the country," Ron's gentle, but masculine voice said. "It's important to me that you see it. I've wanted to show it to you for so long."

"For so long? Does it seem I've been here that long?" Margaret responded, trying to lighten the conversation, trying to cover her emotions.

Ron's tone became very serious. "Do you think your appearing like this has only just awakened my memory of you? You've been part of my life ever since Christmas Eve 1963."

Margaret was truly shocked; yet she knew she'd felt the same way. She was fairly certain she would wake up somewhere, sometime, and find out that she was having an extended dream. Perhaps she had fallen, hit her head and was really in a coma right now. She pinched her arm to see if she could feel it. She could.

A chill went down her spine to think that for twenty years someone had held her that closely in his thoughts; particularly uncanny was that she'd been doing the same. Tears filled the rims of her eyes and trickled down her cheeks. She cried softly for what could have been...perhaps what should have been.

Chapter 10

The house was alive with activity early the next morning. Bill had come to take her mother out and had brought some friends with him. Ann was rushing to get ready as she'd overslept. And Margaret herself was standing bleary-eyed in the kitchen holding a steaming mug of coffee.

"You're going where?" she asked her mother.

"I'm sorry," her mother apologized for about the fifth time. "We made these plans long before Dorothy died. Bill and I made the date with the Hoffsingers to go skiing. We rented a place up at Deep Creek. Since neither of us thought to cancel, we're kind of stuck. I'm so sorry...and you've come all this way."

"Don't worry about me, Mom. I told you before it was all right. Just give me a phone number where you can be reached and don't stay out late," she joked.

"But are you sure you wouldn't like to come with us?"

"No. Well, I mean...thank you for asking. You know how I feel about skiing."

Ann Wood examined her daughter's face carefully. "You're meeting Ron again, aren't you?"

Margaret took a sip of her coffee. "Yes, I am." There was silence for a few moments, while Bill discretely left the room.

"Do you think that it's wise for you to be alone here with an old boyfriend."

"Mom, I'm forty years old."

"I'm sixty two," Ann said. "So what?"

"OK," Margaret said, plopping onto a kitchen chair with her back to the large picture window that overlooked the backyard redwood deck. "What do you want me to say? That I used to be in love with Ron? That was years ago. I was still in my teens. And seeing him again is fun, yes, I'll admit that. Even flattering to my ego that he might still like me just a little, but you have to know well enough how committed I am to my family."

"To your family, yes. And to your marriage?"

Margaret cast a disparaging glance at her mother.

"Are you going to tell Ron about Brent?"

Margaret drew herself up to her full height, her mouth tightened. Her mother always suspected Brent was Ron's baby, not Jerry's, and accused her angrily of it shortly after Brent was born prematurely. It was probably the only time in her life Margaret refused to let herself be intimidated by her mother and she insisted that the matter was closed. Ann hadn't mentioned it for years. Now her mother made it clear it was still her belief that Ron had fathered Brent.

"There is nothing to tell him," Margaret said tersely.

Ann Wood shrugged. "Perhaps not," she admitted, turning to leave. "But I would remind you of one thing. You have only spoken about loving someone once since being here, and it was in connection to Ron, not your family. Be careful." With that, the older woman was out the door with Bill and the Hoffsingers.

Margaret stared after them, feeling at once chagrinned and scolded, always the way her mother managed to make her feel when they disagreed. She poured herself a cup of coffee. There was nothing to be careful of, she thought defiantly. Any kind of relationship with Ron was impossible regardless of feelings. Jerry and the children were constantly in the shadow of her mind. But her heart was playing tricks on her, telling her that Jerry would accept this wonderful relationship with an old friend.

Not long after her mother had left, Margaret showered and dressed, pulling on an ankle-length, black wool skirt, warm, ribbed stockings, and layered a loose burgundy turtleneck sweater over a long-sleeved white silk shell under which she wore a camisole. Waiting for Ron, she checked herself in the ornate living room mirror and pushed her curls into place. How often years ago she had stood in exactly this spot waiting for Ron.

There were still several inches of snow on the ground, but the roads were well-cleared. It was a beautiful sight. Again bringing to mind the Christmas twenty years before when she and Ron had fallen in love.

Twenty years, she thought grimly. Two decades.

Ron's car was immaculate, just as he was. When he opened the door for her, she stepped completely into his world. As she sat, their eyes locked for perhaps a second longer than necessary.

For the second time in their short reunion, the couple headed west toward the Blue Ridge Mountains, which lay fifty miles northwest. They rode in silence for some time, during which Margaret was able to still her pulse and steady her mind. She was as nervous as if this were her first date. Ron also seemed nervous.

"You're quiet; why?" Ron reached over and placed his large hand over hers. At his touch, her heart jumped into her throat.

Suburbs quickly turned to country and the sun glistened on the remaining snow. As they drove on, Margaret was constantly aware of his hand on hers. She sat frozen to the spot, unwilling to move even though her fingers began to cramp. *There would be time;* she told herself, *for my cramped fingers to recover; plenty of time, when this ride became just another memory.*

"How far is your house?" she finally asked, as they took a sharp left turn off the main road and began winding their way through the small town of Battlefront on the west side of the mountain range.

"Not far now," he responded, pulling down the visor against the brilliant sun that streamed in the front window. The farther west they headed, the less tense Ron seemed, Margaret thought.

The small town disappeared into countryside, dotted with houses in very bad repair. Even the little country stores were shabby reminders of years gone by. With the starkness of winter, the world seemed barren.

Cattle, seemingly oblivious to the cars rolling past just feet away, munched bales of hay spread out in the field before them by their caretakers. In another field, large black crows waddled about among the corn stubble calling noisily to one another.

"Is that snow again?" Margaret asked, thinking she saw little white flakes hitting the windshield.

Ron nodded. "I think we're supposed to get a little more today, but the weather's too warm for it to amount to much. Probably will turn to rain."

"Too warm!" Margaret laughed.

Ron laughed too. "It's funny how our definition of 'warm' changes from August to December!"

"Oh, I hope it doesn't snow much," she said, trying to suppress a feeling of panic concerning the possibility of not getting back to her mother's house tonight.

Margaret thought Ron looked disappointed at her comment, but the look was quickly replaced by his cheerful countenance. "Well, let's just find a weather report." He removed his hand from hers and twiddled with the radio. He found an all-news station and they listened in silence while waiting for a weather forecast, which when it came on, informed them that there was a system of snow that would move in north of the area, seemingly missing that part of Virginia altogether.

Ron laughed a delightful, hearty laugh. "Well, that means we'll probably get a foot! Maybe I'd better take you back home right now!"

Margaret managed a nervous smile.

Ron squeezed her hand. "Come on, don't worry," he said. "I'm a good driver and I promise you're safe with me." He winked.

Yes, Margaret thought. I'm safe with Ron. But there were so many questions. What has he been doing for these past two decades? Did he plan to marry Alice? Anyone? Did he live alone? Did he have any contact with his former wife and child? Who was Ron Crenshaw now?

"Ron," she said softly, building her courage. "We need to talk." Ron looked over at her and lingered a bit too long, as he suddenly had to swerve to stay in his own lane. "Yes, we do. But not now," he said quickly regaining control of the car. "Not in the car."

Ron's house was a very large Victorian mansion on a quiet street in a little town nestled between two mountain ranges. It had taken nearly two hours to get there. The snow had begun falling heavily, covering the melting mounds of dirty snow that lingered from the last storm, and frosting the trees. It made the house look like a picture postcard.

Margaret observed that Ron was a caring house-owner, at least judging by the perfect order of the outside of the house. The paint was bright; the porch clean and tidy, shrubs were protected from the weather by burlap. Inside the house was so precisely decorated it had the look of a model home in a new housing development, with perfectly placed plants and not a cup or glass to be seen. Tapestry pillows accented the furniture that looked brand new—not tainted by teenaged sweat socks or spilled soft drinks. There was not a book out of place on the neatly organized bookshelves that ran floor to ceiling in the library. Not at all like Margaret's house, where most of the time books and papers filled tables, athletic shoes graced every bit of floor space, and loose clothing was trapped like a magnet to any available chair. There were no pets here; no signs of animal hair or odor that plagued Margaret every time one of the kids brought home another cat or dog, which they had done frequently throughout the years.

Ron proudly took Margaret on a tour of his hundred-year-old, four-story dwelling and detailed the renovations he had done, apparently by himself.

On the second floor was a large master bedroom, which was Ron's, he told her. To make it the size he wanted, he had taken out a non-bearing wall between two smaller bedrooms, which gave him enough space to put in a modern bathroom with stall shower and Jacuzzi. An elaborate office was set up in an alcove off the bedroom. That was where he displayed his antique gun collection.

"Do you still hunt?" Margaret said, observing the number of guns in a somewhat crowded space.

Ron shook his head. "Not like I used to. Once in a while Dad asks me to go, but we don't do it often. Too hard on him and frankly I don't have the time. I keep the guns up here because one of my roommates doesn't want them downstairs."

"Roommate?"

"Yes, Joe. He has the entire third floor," Ron said. "He's in town this week, which is unusual, so you might meet him later. And Alice lives here. You met her at Dad's house after the funeral. She has an apartment in the basement. It's an English basement, though, so it's a walkout basement and she has windows. It's pretty nice down there."

"It's so—organized. I'd never have known three people lived here!"

"Thank you," Ron smiled at her. "I'll take that as a compliment as I'm most often the housekeeper. They both have jobs that keep them on the road, so I'm alone most of the time!"

Margaret watched Ron's face as he went on about the house and its history. His was such a kind face; plain, yet elegant. Strong. But who was he? It had been too long since she'd felt like she knew him...and now she wondered if she ever really knew the man at all. Standing here in his house, learning bits about his life, she realized that they had become virtual strangers. The people they were twenty years before had gone on, experiencing life quite differently. There was indeed something very mysterious about him. Despite his apparent openness, there seemed to be always something left unsaid, some postscript he was saving for later. She was so deep in thought she did not realize immediately that Ron had asked her a question and was now staring intently into her eyes waiting for an answer. How long, she wondered, had she been just staring blankly back at him? She knew they were speaking to each other through their eyes, but what were they saying? What, especially, did he think she was saying to him? Her chest felt heavy, she was a bit afraid, yet it was a wonderful experience to be so totally engulfed in someone else.

Without warning a strange man blew through the front door, two overstuffed briefcases in tow, brushing snow off his coatless shoulders.

"Cold!" he exclaimed directly to Margaret, extending his hand. "You must be Margaret." He was businesslike and formal.

Ron grinned. "Margaret, you may have guessed. This is Joe."

"Hi, Joe," she said, quickly removing her hand from the cold one that held hers. "I've been admiring your lovely house."

Immediately Joe set down his briefcases. "If you two are planning to go out, you'd better make it a short evening; it's a mess out there."

Ron went to the window and peered out. Indeed the snow was falling heavily, covering roads and grass alike. "We have reservations for six o'clock at The Country Inn." Ron checked his watch. "It's nearly five now. Why don't we head there now and see if we can get an earlier table. I'm sure the snow will have let up by then and the plows will have cleared the roads in an hour or so."

Margaret felt a sense of foreboding as Ron helped her into her coat. Soon they were on their way through the snow that fell in large, soft flakes against the windshield.

The Country Inn was a beautiful place, a 200-year-old fieldstone structure reached by way of a quaint covered bridge over a branch of the Shenandoah River. It had been an Inn continuously since the early 1700s. The food was served family style by waiters dressed in period costume; the atmosphere relaxed and homey. This was a place where one could dress up or down and still be correct. It was dark in the candlelit dining area, but Margaret's eyes gradually grew accustomed to the warm glow. The waiter, who seemed to know Ron well, seated Ron and Margaret near the oversized stone fireplace in which a large hot fire was burning giant logs.

"See anything you like, or shall I order for you?" Ron offered, glancing over his menu at Margaret.

"Order for me, you probably know what's good." She glanced around the quaint old room; which made her long for an earlier, less complicated time. In a split second, she imagined herself in a floor-length Colonial dress and Ron in coattails.

He ordered her a drink, then perused the menu. Unaccustomed to having drinks before dinner, Margaret immediately felt the relaxing effect of the alcohol. Though it made her cheeks flushed, she was grateful to finally have her nerves settle down. She watched Ron as he read the menu, casually sipping his drink, apparently completely at ease. But she was not at all at ease. There was a very real awareness within her that she was in a strange restaurant in a strange town with a man she was beginning to realize was truly a stranger—a stranger who had an undeniable power over her.

When the attentive waiter returned, Ron ordered for both of them, then, before releasing the waiter, waited for Margaret's approval of the choice of meal. She nodded and blushed as he smiled at her as if she belonged to him. She could not pull her eyes away from his any more than she had been able to pull away from his embrace at the funeral. Her heart pounded slowly, steadily, but hard against her chest. She was, she realized, very happy. She determined to relish the moment, to make the most of the little time they had together. Then she would go home and move on...

Finally unable to take the intense feeling of his constant gaze, she fumbled through her mind for something to say.

"Is your father still keeping up that cheerful front?"

"He's doing fine. Did you know your cheeks are bright red? Are we too close to the fire?"

She shook her head. Reality again. Ron kept bringing reality into the scene and she just wanted to languish in make-believe. Her whole life had been reality—cold, hard "do it the right way" reality. From marrying Jerry as soon as she realized a baby was coming, to sticking with him through women like Abigail. For the time being, she just wanted to pretend she was someone else.

Ron set his glass down and took both her hands in his. "Where are you Margaret?"

Margaret nervously withdrew her hands and finished her drink quickly.

Ron tilted his chair back on two legs. "You haven't changed," he stated. "Still shy. Still that quiet little girl who hides within herself. What secrets are locked in there, beautiful lady?" he asked, touching her temple gently.

Though she didn't think it possible, Margaret's cheeks got redder. Over the past twenty years she'd felt anything but beautiful. There had been a time when she thought she was attractive, but that time passed quickly as she became a mother and so involved in little lives that she hardly had time to keep up her appearance. "Thank you," she whispered.

"Don't thank me," he chuckled. "I had nothing to do with your good looks."

"Oh, it's just that sometimes I feel so darn old."

Ron shook his head. "You will never be anything but beautiful, because your beauty is inside. But it's more than that, Margaret. I see the heart you have always managed to hide. I see the girl that lives inside the woman; the girl who used to wade barefoot in the creek with me and chase minnows. You weren't even afraid of snakes and turtles!"

It was a world upside down; she was turned inside out.

Their meal came, along with a bottle of wine. Ron had ordered well; the meal was superb. Margaret couldn't remember when she had felt so special or been treated so gently. And at last, with the help of the warm fire and the strong wine, she was able to relax and enjoy the moment.

After dinner, they refused dessert and turned their chairs to better view the fireplace, leaning back drowsily in the warmth of the crackling flames, enjoying the remainder of the wine.

"OK," Ron said, breaking the long silence between them. "I've been rude about your life long enough. Tell me about your kids."

Margaret was so unprepared for that question that she nearly swallowed the wrong way. "My kids?" Reality again.

"Yes," Ron said, leaning forward. "You have three I believe."

"Yes, yes I do." Margaret said, dabbing her mouth with the linen napkin and replacing it in her lap. "Brent, Jason and Susan."

"Ages?"

"Well, Susan is my baby. She's just become a teenager. She's an artist."

"Does she look like her mother?"

"Better," Margaret smiled coquetishly, hurrying quickly on. "Then there's Jason; he's sixteen and he's a real jock. Loves any kind of ball. And Brent, my oldest, is in college."

"Really? Where?"

"University of Virginia, as a matter of fact. That can't be too far from here."

"It's not. About three hours. Maybe less. Want to drive down there."

Margaret's eyes opened wide. "You must be joking."

"No. If you want to go, I'll take you."

Margaret shook her head. "No, he's in the middle of exams. I'll see him when he gets home."

"So is he enjoying his first year as a college man?"

"This is his second year. Brent's nearly twenty."

Ron's face registered mild surprise, and though he said nothing, Margaret felt the need to hurry on. "He's about to be engaged."

"Young for that. Tell me more about him."

"Like what?"

"Well, what's his major?"

"Art," she answered abruptly. "He's an artist like his sister. They're just alike." She didn't want to discuss the children anymore.

"You're upset."

"No—no really. Not upset. Flustered."

Ron smiled as though he understood everything. But he didn't, she assured herself. He couldn't. Margaret tried desperately to find a comfortable place between her real life and the fantasy she wanted this evening to be.

"Anything you want to ask of me?" Ron asked obligingly.

There were so many questions. Margaret looked into Ron's sparkling eyes and tried to calm down. Talking about the children confused her emotions. Here, in this place, with Ron...the children seemed a million miles away. And just for tonight, that's what she wanted. This was her moment, and though it would be fleeting, she grasped at it.

She pondered over what question could she ask Ron that would not take away for the magic of this moment together? "No questions just now...maybe there are so many I don't know where to start. This place is so wonderful, it makes me feel transported as though nothing else exists..."

Clearly he understood.

"Tell me about the Inn," she asked. Ron easily accommodated her, having not only the history down pat, but little vignettes—stories about Indian raids in the 1700s and loyal slaves who had kept the Inn from burning by the Yankee Army passing through during the Civil War. He mentioned one of his brothers who had worked for a time at the Inn, and from there began talking about his family. He related so many stories Margaret found it hard to keep up with who was who.

Then Ron began to talk about his mother. At first he retained complete control of his emotions as he reminisced. He embarked on a dissertation all the way back to the days when he and Margaret played together as little children, remembering with much laughter the time when his mother had "rescued" them when they got away from her on a visit to Theodore Roosevelt Island. He talked about what a good grandmother she was, how his mother had loved to cook, how well she could sew, how many friends she had. He began laughing as he shared amusing anecdotes of her life, but quickly the uncontrollable laughter turned to tears. He leaned forward, covering his face with both hands.

"I'm sorry," he choked, shoulders shaking.

"Ron..." she whispered, her heart breaking for him. She reached across the table to touch his arm. He gripped her hand as he fought to regain composure.

"I miss her, Margaret. There was so much left unresolved. So many things we didn't say to each other. I almost can't stand it. It hurts so much."

"I know...I really know. I still miss my father like that. The pain doesn't stop, but it does become bearable." She moved her chair closer to his and slipped her arm around him. Tears burned her own eyes and crept down her cheeks. "No, Margaret, you couldn't possibly know," Ron blurted out. "All your life, you've done the right thing. I have not. And though I suspect my mother knew that, I never talked with her about it. And I wanted to. Oh, God, how I wanted to talk things out with her. But I was a coward. I let her die without explaining..." Ron's voice trailed off as he pursed his lips and made a strong attempt to recover his emotions.

Margaret remembered what Cathy had told her about there being some rumor about trouble he might have been involved in. But whatever it was, Ron wasn't a criminal. She tried hard to empathize. "Ron, I'm sure...no, I know—your mother loved and accepted you unconditionally. Whatever you feel you wanted to explain probably didn't matter to her."

"Maybe, Margaret. Maybe—" Ron was cut off abruptly when the room went dark. Margaret glanced at her watch. It was nearly 11 p.m. and they hadn't looked out the window for more than an hour. Now, in the dimly lit room, she was reminded that there had been a heavy snow falling. She stood up and cupped her hands against a window to see out. Then to everyone's relief, then the lights flickered and came back on.

"Sorry folks," the owner of the restaurant said, appearing in the doorway. "There's a line down somewhere, but we have a generator. However, we've just had word that the police have closed the road between here and the main road due to a fallen tree that took down power lines. Apparently lines are down everywhere, so it's going to be some time before they get to the back roads. If you would like accommodations, we have a few rooms available. And there's plenty of room down here with the staff. Drinks on the house!"

"Don't worry," Ron said hurriedly responding to Margaret's very worried look. "I'll take care of this."

Margaret excused herself and found the ladies' room. She washed her hands and splashed water on her face, really frightened that she wouldn't be able to get back home tonight. When she headed back to the table, she discovered Ron coming out of the bar.

"I thought there wasn't going to be any more snow," she cried.

"It seems a weather system they thought would miss us has stalled over us," he said grimly. "There's no way we're leaving here tonight. My car would make it, but this heavy wet snow has brought trees down everywhere. We're literally blocked in." His words were slow and deliberate.

How glad Margaret was that her mother and Bill were away for the night. This would be something to try to explain.

"The good news is we can stay here tonight. The bad news is there's only one room left." Ron watched her carefully.

"One room!" Margaret's voice was telling.

"So I'll get you settled, then come back down here and play cards with Roger and the waiters."

"Why only one room?"

"Well, this is a relatively small inn, they already had some overnight guests scheduled, and there were several diners who booked before I had a chance."

"I don't feel right about you staying down here all alone. Why don't I just plan to stay down here too and we can watch the snow together. Let someone else have the room."

"Don't be silly. I enjoy Roger; we go way back. Come on, let's at least look at the room."

Ron took Margaret's hand and led her up a long, steep staircase, around the corner and to the end of the hall. There was a door standing open and inside Margaret could see one double bed, a dresser and a chair. They stepped inside and the room was freezing.

"I'll go find out if there's a way to get some heat up here," Ron whispered. Whispering seemed appropriate in the quaint darkened inn.

The small room, which was directly at the front of the inn, overlooked a cobblestone street, which led to a few outbuildings that had once housed horses and other livestock, and a blacksmith's shop. They were beautifully adorned for Christmas with lights and evergreens, but with the Inn running only on a generator, only the light of the moon shining through the breaking clouds illuminated them. Not a footprint disturbed the smooth silent whiteness. She stood for a long time absorbing the stillness, thinking that the first Christmas might well have been a night like this. She shivered. The cold began to permeate her thick winter coat.

In a few minutes Ron returned with an elderly bearded man carrying a load of kindling in one arm and a tote bag in the other. Behind him was another man who carried an armload of wood. Turning to leave quickly, one of the men handed Ron the tote bag, which contained a bottle of wine, fresh fruit, cheese and a loaf of French bread. "Compliments of the management," he said, bowing cordially as he left.

Ron began to make the fire. He skillfully laid the kindling in place, then struck a match. While the flames crackled as they devoured the kindling and began to attack the dry logs, Ron poured each of them a glass of wine. "To you," he said, lifting his glass and touching it to hers. "And to what you mean to me." He took a long drink of the burgundy colored liquid. "Would you like to dance?"

"Dance?" Margaret looked at him in disbelief.

"Thought it might warm you," he said with a twinkle in his eye. "Don't you hear the music Miss Wood?" He cupped his hand to his ear as if straining to hear something in the distance.

"Well, yes, I believe I do," she pretended along with him, setting her glass on the table and walking into his arms.

Margaret's head swirled as she fit her body next to his. He held her so tightly she could hardly breathe, yet she did not want him to loosen his grasp.

Quietly, he began to hum, his body easily leading her as he gently moved to his own music. Weak, she needed him to hold her tightly now so that she didn't collapse on unstable legs. When he pressed his lips against her cheek, his body began to tremble. She could feel the vibrations of the tune he was humming as he held his mouth against her ear, still humming a vaguely familiar tune. Now in a trance-like state, she was totally swept away. She wanted to remain that way forever. It felt too wonderful; too much of a dream realized. She was holding the man she had loved so long. Life as Margaret Ammons had known it came to a stand still. The moment was ethereal—two people sharing a lost moment in time.

For a while their bodies swayed in place to the tempo of the music only the two of them could hear, then slowly Ron began to move her around the room, singing the words to a love song. His voice was low, sultry

"Even now," he sang, his lips still pressed against her ear, "Even now when I have come so far I wonder where you are, I wonder why it's still so hard without you..."

Margaret floated in his arms, feeling so secure and loved. It vaguely bothered her that she didn't know what it was that he hadn't told his mother that plagued him so. Her mind kept asking the question as if trying to warn her but she wasn't hearing.

Ron's mouth moved away from her ear where the heat of his breath left a cool, moist area. He sought her lips. "May I," he murmured, as his lips touched hers briefly, then he simply held her tightly again and, with sudden fancy footwork, swirled her in a complete circle.

"I'd better go downstairs now," he whispered hoarsely, and Margaret reluctantly released her grasp of him. She held onto his hand and when he went to pull away, she gripped it more tightly. His eyes questioned hers. He drew in a deep breath. "Margaret, please. I want to stay...more than anything. But I don't want to hurt you. I'd better go."

She knew he was right, but still she could not release his hand. As they stood, eyes locked together, she took an imperceptible step closer to him. Instantly he engulfed her in his arms. "I love you, Margaret," he buried his face in her hair. "I truly love you."

Tears rolled down her cheeks; tears for the girl long ago who had so wanted to hear those words from him then; tears for the woman she was now who could never know the kind of love he might have been able to give her. "If only you'd said so..."

"Don't cry, Sweetheart." He kissed her forehead and looked woeful. "I couldn't tell you back then, I was too devastated by losing my wife and daughter...too afraid if I let myself love you, I'd be hurt again. Not a day has gone by that you haven't been on my mind. When something good happens, I want to tell you. When something bad happens, I want to lessen my burden by sharing it with you. It's like that song I was singing you. It's about us.

"My life has taken a strange road since we parted, but I hope you will always believe that every inch of that road, you've been uppermost in my heart...

"I want you Margaret," he breathed softly. His breathing became labored. "I can be your lover, or I can be your friend. But no matter what happens here tonight, my love for you won't change.

"But it's your decision."

She drew in a quick breath. He was giving her a choice...asking her to make the decision. She turned away from his hypnotic eyes. Why couldn't it be simpler than this? Why didn't he force himself on her...give her an excuse for giving in to the feelings that were overpowering her? Then she could place the blame, if there ever was blame to be placed; she could make excuses to herself the rest of her life if necessary. Yes, she wanted him to make love to her; but could she say it?

Her head pounded with the thought "make a choice, make a choice." Her insides shouted "choose love," yet she couldn't. It was better if he left; better if they could somehow go back to their own lives and simply hold tonight as a special memory forever hidden in their hearts. She knew Ron was reading her thoughts. She wondered if he could possibly tell how much she longed just to lose herself in his arms.

"I'm going to go now," he said, clearing his throat and taking steps away from her. Slowly, very slowly as if expecting her to resist him, he reached out to her and lowered his lips over hers. Time stopped. There was no longer any clear thought process, only a primal longing. He slipped a strong arm around her and walked her over to the bed. He sat tentatively beside her, his eyes searching hers, begging, pleading for a response. There was no hesitation. She reached her arms around his neck and pulled him toward her.

She was no longer Margaret Ammons; he was no longer Ron Crenshaw. Now they were every couple who had ever been in love; every couple who had ever been parted and come together again; every couple who ever longed for a second chance.

Chapter 11

Jerry Ammons stood at the pay phone in Palm Beach Airport holding the receiver indecisively in his hand. He should call his mother and tell her he'd arrived safely, but he didn't want to have to listen to her complaining. Suddenly Abigail appeared from the ladies room, lipstick and hair renewed to perfection.

"Did you get through to your kids?" she asked.

Jerry just nodded and hung up the receiver. He'd call later.

"Are the kids giving your mother any problem?"

Jerry grunted and checked his watch. "We'd better get going; we've only got a few hours before the dinner."

It felt good to step outside the airport into the warm Florida air; good to get away from winter...and his mother. There wasn't much time before Margaret would be back home, either. He needed to make the most of this trip. He'd been thwarted at his attempts with Abigail one too many times.

Tall palm trees swayed gently against a clear, blue sky as Jerry and Abigail jumped into the nearest cab and headed for Singer Island where they planned to meet seventeen men and women from various computer firms. These people were meeting surreptitiously to form their own company. It was a top-secret expedition. These people were the creative forces behind much of what went on in their current companies; the planners—the dreamers coming together with the ones who could make those plans and dreams work. Now they had found each other, found common ground. And they were a disgruntled group. In their own eyes, underpaid and under-appreciated. But they had no idea how to begin to change things. Jerry had agreed to help them form their company. His own attorney would be there to give the necessary legal advice. Jerry looked forward to the adventure; he especially looked forward to the possibilities ahead with Abigail. Ever since that frustrating evening at the Simpsons when Charles showed up, Jerry had been longing for another chance with her. He'd been distant lately, strictly professional, thinking another tactic might be in order. It proved to be a good move on his part, as Abigail seemed a lot more attentive. But right now, that was not what was on his mind. He needed to sort his thoughts out before he stood before this group and presented the plans.

It didn't take Jerry long to settle into his large comfortable suite. He hung his garment bag in the closet, unpacked his toiletries and underwear, and then slipped into his swimming trunks and polo shirt. He glanced at the telephone and punched 213. "Abigail?" he asked to make sure he had dialed the right number. "Let's go down to the beach for an hour."

In moments, Abigail was knocking on the door between their rooms. "You didn't have to ring…you could have just knocked on the door!" she laughed when she came through.

"I could have," Jerry smiled, fully appreciating her long, slim legs, which showed beneath her short, lacey cover-up.

Together they strolled along the beach at the edge of the water, letting it lap at their feet. Coming from cold wet weather to the warmth of Florida was like a balm to the soul. Jerry let the sun warm his face as he tried to totally relax. Though Abigail kept trying to close the space between them, Jerry kept his distance. Now was not the time to be distracted. There was never anything that stood between Jerry and his work. Not even Abigail. He had to be the best at what he did; he was his own hardest critic. Or was it perhaps the echo of his father's voice always pushing him to achieve more?

Thirty minutes down the beach and thirty back left them just enough time to take a dip in the indoor pool, which was too warm for Jerry but Abigail found perfect. For a moment, Jerry stood watching Abigail gracefully crawl the length of the pool and back, then he closed his eyes and turned his thoughts to the meeting. He had his notes, his transparencies and a copy of the complete report for each individual. He had prepared his talk and had a written agreement for each to sign. The income this deal would produce would be great if this new company got off the ground, and it should. Computers were the future.

"Sleeping?" Abigail laughed as she treaded water near him.

"Not sleeping," he said, staring fully into her large, blue eyes. "Planning." Jerry hoped this little outing would not be a detriment to his thought process at the evening meeting. It was his custom not to let anything get in the way of work and as much as he wanted to have time alone with Abigail, he wondered if it had been a mistake to bring her along. If things went right here, it could be big money.

Back in his room, Jerry hung up his towel and bathing suit and quickly stepped into a cold shower.

It was exactly seven o'clock when Jerry entered the spacious dining room of the Singer Island Camelot. A youthful forty-one, he cut a dashing figure in his expensive, dark suit, his thick dark hair neatly trimmed, his square jaw set. He became aware of someone at his elbow. He swung around, halfway expecting to see Abigail, but it was J.D. Harkins.

"J.D.—you got here! How're you doing?"

"Great, now that I'm here. Glad to get out of the frozen north! Are you here with the family?"

"Nope, not when I have to work, J.D."

"What a shame you couldn't bring them here. This is just what a body needs. We're snowed in at home. Terrible storm in Washington. Knocked out power all around. I had trouble getting to the airport."

"Really? My wife's visiting her mother there."

"In D.C.?"

"Nearby."

"Well, she got snowed in then."

Jerry pondered Margaret having to stay longer because of the storm. He wondered if his mother could take it. "I'll tell you what," he said, "having Margaret away from home for nearly a week already sure makes me appreciate her."

"Margaret...your wife's name is Margaret?" J.D.'s eyes held a faraway look. "Of course," he said as if a light bulb went off. "Margaret Ammons..."

"Right. I think you met her at last year's Christmas party—oh, no, she didn't come. She was ill." The two men headed into the private dining room together. There a group of what seemed to Jerry to be very young people sat chatting among themselves. All the chatter stopped as soon as the two men entered.

"Let's order a round of drinks and introduce ourselves," Jerry said, sitting at the head of the table. "Then let's get this show on the road!"

Despite its dubious beginnings, trying to work with people who were half his age in an area in which he was completely unfamiliar, the evening was a success for Jerry. His attorney was well accepted. J.D. Harkins agreed to be a straw for those present who were not yet free to add their names to the company roster. Abigail was professional, taking copious notes, and, as always, looked stunning, though Jerry hardly noticed her. Things went so well, he could hardly believe it. This would be the business deal that would make all of them millionaires, perhaps many times over.

Back in his hotel suite, Abigail poured Jerry a drink as he fell on the couch and loosened his tie. "My head is still spinning with all that computer mumbo-jumbo," he said. "It's disconcerting to be leading a business deal when you don't know what the other parties are talking about." He accepted the drink. "Still," he added philosophically, "I don't need to know the details; I'm just the glue making it all stick together." He was clearly proud of himself.

"So everyone was happy?" Abigail asked, sitting down beside him.

"Not J.D. Though he went along fine, something I said earlier must have stuck in his craw. He got very distant and avoided any one-on-one with me."

"Maybe that's just his business persona."

Jerry shook his head. "Nope. I've known J.D. several years and we've done deals together many times." He looked over at the woman sitting beside him. "You know, if I had to guess, I'd say he was hoping to spend some time with you. You'd distract anybody."

To Jerry's surprise, Abigail laughed out loud. "I very much doubt it, Jerry."

Jerry frowned, not understanding her attitude at all. "Oh, come on, Abigail. You can't be so naïve as to think you don't stop traffic!"

"Jerry, sometimes I think you have only one thing on your mind. I'm more than what you see on the outside, you know."

Jerry had heard women take this stance before and he knew he was treading on dangerous ground. Women liked to be attractive to men, he knew, but they also had to think men were interested in their intellect. "You're right. And J.D.'s a smart man. He'd definitely be the type to notice you're not only beautiful, but intelligent and extremely capable." He put his arm around her, not particularly liking the direction the conversation was taking. Obviously pleased at his response, she smiled, her face inches from his. "Jerry, J.D. may think I'm beautiful and smart. But trust me, he's *not* interested."

"OK, I'll bite. Why not?"

"Darling," Abigail said, touching her lips to his. "J.D. Harkins is gay."

Chapter 12

Ron Crenshaw sat in his living room transfixed by the music he'd loaded into his elaborate stereo. The room was dark, except in the far corner where a gooseneck lamp shone down on the newspaper Joe was studying in-depth, his reading glasses low on his nose. Once in a while he glanced over at Ron, trying to decide what was bothering him, but he only knew the man was deep in thought. It worried him. He wished Alice would come home. She was always able to get Ron talking when he got in these moods, which happened more often over the past months. Since Margaret Ammons went back to Indiana over a week ago, Ron had been almost incommunicable. Joe didn't like what he was thinking, but it seemed the only answer. Margaret had been one of his girlfriends, but that had been at least twenty years before. Joe thought Ron should have been able to shake it off by now. Particularly since she was married with children.

Where was Alice anyway? Joe knew Alice could take much of the credit for Ron's recovery after his nervous breakdown. She had nursed him back; the voice of reason in a world that had turned confusing and disoriented for Ron.

"Where's Alice?" Joe asked as casually as possible.

"No idea," Ron responded, not looking up. He thought of Alice briefly then, remembering how loyal she'd been, obsessively so, ever since he'd gotten sick. In the years since, all three of them had settled into a comfortable routine of living together, and yet managing quite separate lives. But Ron didn't kid himself; he was inextricably entwined here, and to pretend differently would be a lie.

He hadn't been able to tell Margaret about that and hoped he'd never have to. She'd go back to her life with husband and children and hopefully never look back. Would she keep in touch? She'd been so quiet on their return to her mother's house; Ron imagined she was regretting their time together. If he'd caused her any kind of a problem, he'd never forgive himself. *I should have been stronger,* Ron thought bitterly. All he could hope for was that she wouldn't grow to hate him.

"Let's go out for a bite," Joe suggested, pulling the newspaper together and removing his reading glasses.

Ron didn't respond immediately and Joe wondered for a moment if he'd even heard. The man had such a way of escaping into himself. It was as though he was living somewhere else, in a private world. Alice indicated he was possessed by a memory—a ghost she had called it. Up until Ron's mother died, he seemed to have recovered from that escapism; perhaps that was what the problem was. Still struggling with his mother's death. "Come on, let's go grab some dinner," Joe repeated.

"I'm not hungry," Ron said flatly, still staring at the wall where the stereo was playing. "I had a snack just a little while ago."

"You mean that banana? That was three hours ago." Joe stood up and stretched. "Come on. If you're not hungry, at least come with me and keep me company. I hate eating along."

Though the mention of food made Ron's stomach growl, he didn't care. He was thinking about Margaret, and he had enough experience with life to know that if he didn't replay the scenes over and over, they would soon fade. Right now, when he thought of her, he could feel her in his arms, taste her, and smell her light perfume. Would he be able to remember all this next week? Next month? How, he wondered miserably, could he go on without her.

For a fleeting moment, he wished he'd have been more forceful; maybe she would have agreed to leave her family…then he scolded himself for thinking so selfishly. Margaret knew so little about him.

Whatever love she had for him was based on the Ron she thought she knew, the Ron he had been all those years before. She didn't know the Ron who'd emerged during the ensuing years. He hoped she never would.

The drive back to her mother's house had been too quick. There had been no time to say what he knew he had to say if they were to continue any kind of relationship. But there was no kind of relationship they could have. He'd never heard of two people loving each other for so long without ever having been in touch. Regardless, the circumstances of their separate lives meant that there was no future for them. He would have to love her within, where there was no space or time. Now, with her memory so fresh in his brain, reality told him it would be best to file the memories away and let her go. If he could.

With the great precision that comes from much practice, he turned knobs and shut down his stereo, then went to the hall to get his coat. "Let's go," he said, heading to the door.

"Where to?" Joe asked cheerfully, expecting a change of scenery to brighten the mood.

"You're the hungry one," Ron groused. "You know what you want to eat."

Joe was angered but said nothing. He headed the car towards the nearest fast food place, almost hoping Ron would complain since he didn't like fast food at all. At least that would provide a glimmer of hope he was not getting sick again.

The roads were cleared of the heavy wet snow of the previous week. It now lay in dirty piles along the sides of the roads. Tree limbs, large and small, still cluttered fields, and at the shopping center, the snow was in brown mounds piled high to open up places for cars to park so people could get their holiday shopping done.

Joe wheeled into the restaurant and got in line alone while Ron found a table. Joe ordered one of the specials; Ron only wanted coffee.

"Oh, for God's sake," Joe muttered. "I don't know what's eating you, but it will survive longer than you will if you don't put food inside yourself. You want to go somewhere else?"

Ron looked angrily at the man before him. "I don't know why the hell you think you've been appointed my guardian, but you can shut up and leave me alone."

Joe stared long and hard across the table, many responses on his mind, but he said nothing. He turned his attention to his food, for which Ron was grateful. All he wanted to do was slip into the memories of his short time in Margaret's arms. It had been so long since he'd held a woman; he'd forgotten how soft and vulnerable they were. He knew, though, that it wasn't just because he held a woman, but because it was Margaret.

He sipped his coffee pensively, giving the appearance of studying people as they came and went from the restaurant, but actually he was so deep in thought he saw no one. His every thought was of Margaret and how her reappearance had turned his life upside down...a life that he had learned to accept, had settled into. She couldn't know that she had made chaos out of what had taken him so long to put in order. But it didn't matter. She had heightened his senses; made him feel alive again. It had taken years of therapy for him to feel good about himself and the life he'd chosen after she married Jerry. Years to relegate Margaret to a proper position in his life. It had taken him years to become satisfied with who he had become... Now he was confused again, and it didn't take a rocket scientist to see that Joe suspected that.

Joe chewed his last morsel of food, sloshed it down with a coke and wiped his mouth. "Ready for the week?" he asked, gathering up the trash.

Ron blinked. "The week?"

"Yes, the week ahead... you know, Monday morning. Work."

Ron took another sip of coffee. "I'm as ready as I ever am for Monday."

"I didn't know Monday's ever bothered you."

Ron stood up angrily. "You don't know much about me at all," he seethed. " You know what I want you to know. That's all. Period. And don't ever forget that."

"Hey, man. I don't know what's eating you, but I was only making conversation."

"Great. Thanks," Ron replied, "Now let's get the hell out of here." Back in the car Ron slammed the door and lit a cigarette. "I told you I didn't want to come. You should have left me alone."

Joe turned the key in the ignition, anger burning. Finally he'd had enough. "I've spent fifteen years looking after you... You sonofabitch!" he shouted.

Instantly Ron had Joe by the front of the shirt, drawing his fist up in a tight ball. He was shaking with anger. "You can call me anything you want," he hissed. "Except that." Then he slammed Joe back against the seat and searched the floor for the cigarette he had dropped.

Back home, Ron went into the kitchen and poured himself a drink. He couldn't go on feeling like this. It was guilt eating away at him—for what he felt he'd led Margaret to, for the part about himself he hadn't shared with her—just as he hadn't share it with his mother. Ron was pouring his second drink when Joe returned alone.

"Hey, Joe," Ron said when Joe came back through the room. "I just need a little space. I've got some issues... None of it your fault." He started to say more but thought better of it. "I'm going to start back with Sarah Hanson," he said hesitantly. "As soon as I can get an appointment."

"You've worked through all that," Joe said, stopping short in his tracks.

"This is different. And I'm not ready to talk about it."

"That makes a hell of a lot of sense. You're going to see your therapist, but you're not ready to talk about it! What are you going to do? Sit and stare at her? Make her guess what's wrong like the rest of us have to?"

"I mean I don't want to talk about it to you, or Alice or anybody else." Ron drained his drink.

Joe angered again. "It's that woman, isn't it? You spent fifteen years in therapy and you let one stupid wench trash it all?"

"Watch it," Ron threatened, but he was determined not to be

goaded into revealing his feelings about Margaret. "It's been a long time since I had a session," he said, carefully choosing his words. "Sarah told me I'd probably need one from time to time. Well, now's the time."

Deep down, Ron didn't think he needed any therapy. If Margaret weren't attached...if there was no family...if she and he could just go off together and begin life where they had left off; where no one knew them as anything but a couple, he'd never need therapy again. But that wasn't the case. Not now anyway.

Later that night, when Ron was alone in his room he whispered into the darkness. "No matter how many more years go by," he vowed. "We will be together."

Chapter 13

One week before Christmas, finally Margaret felt ready. If it hadn't been for her visit to D.C., she doubted she would have been, her frame of mind had been so bad. Throughout the years, holidays—especially Christmas—seemed to make her more morose. She blamed it on Jerry. The beautiful family stuff that Christmas cards and even television commercials often depicted were a constant reminder that her family didn't have that. Now that she'd been home, to the hometown that stood in the shadow of that wonderful old Catholic church, she knew what was missing, but didn't know how to recapture it. Replacing family moments were the mandatory parties sandwiched in between school basketball games and Jerry's end-of-the-year client "deals" that had to be taken care of before the New Year began. When the children were younger, Christmas Day was a fiasco of trying to get gifts opened, trying to get everybody fed, showered and dressed in time to get over to Jerry's mother's house for a 4 o'clock dinner. Nowadays, it was more likely that the kids wanted to open their gifts and get over to a friend's house to share a new video game or cassette tape of their favorite group. This year she especially felt determined to have at least a few hours of family time during which they at least mentioned what the celebration was all about.

Times had changed, Margaret acknowledged. She didn't necessarily have to go back to the days of "over the river and through the woods to grandmother's," but she longed for a cozy family scene with father, mother and children—grown though they may be—gathered around the tree for more than a quick ripping-off of wrapping paper and comparing who got what. In her house, the "father" seemed to slip in and out so often it was hard to remember year to year if he'd been home at all.

Ron would have been different, Margaret was sure. His strong commitment to family would have made him the kind of father who participated with the family. He wouldn't have let them slip away from the meaning of Christmas.

But she didn't have Ron and she wouldn't. She had Jerry, and instead of wasting all these years wishing things were different, she knew she had to make a change. Especially now that she'd been with Ron. Knowing that he still loved her changed something and she felt like a totally different woman.

Tonight she would go to Susan's Christmas concert, then slip over to Jerry's office for the ever-so-important Christmas party that brought everyone who'd ever had anything to do with the company for miles around. Margaret was surprised to discover that she was actually looking forward to the party. She had been annoyed that Jerry was going straight to the party rather than Susan's concert first, as she was. But then that was Jerry. "You can tape it for me," Jerry had said as he straightened the black bow tie. Anger had risen in Margaret. Without too much trouble, he could do the same as she was doing—go to the concert and still make the party. Before the visit with Ron, she'd have seethed over that the whole evening. But now she felt differently: Jerry had his life, she had hers.

"What is it about you?" Ginny Ashwell asked as the two found a seat together in the middle school auditorium. "Ever since your trip home, you look twenty years younger! And tonight—in that dress you're a knockout." Ginny herself was a beautiful woman. Her nearly black hair was cropped short in a style that flattered her strong facial features. Her intense mahogany eyes were framed with dark eyelashes, played up even more by heavy black eyeliner. Ginny's casual look was always striking whether working in the garden or attending a formal affair. "What happened while you were away?"

Margaret was not prepared for Ginny's insight, and her face immediately reddened. In the ten years they'd known each other, very little escaped Ginny's scrutiny. Now the woman sat grinning as if she already knew the answer to the question.

"Thank you for the compliment," Margaret said trying to sound as nonchalant as possible. "I feel just a little out of place. Not everyone here is dressed for a formal office party, you might have noticed."

"It's more than that," Ginny squinted her eyes and peered into Margaret's. "It's got something to do with that old boyfriend, hasn't it?"

Margaret knew keeping a secret from Ginny, especially one that had changed her so much, would be impossible. The woman had been her best friend since their older boys were in pre-school. They'd shared everything, even stories about past romances. Most people would have forgotten much of what had passed between them in the thousands of conversations they'd had, but not Ginny. She never forgot anything. And clearly she remembered the long afternoon in Margaret's kitchen so many years before while their boys played video games together that Margaret shared the story of Ron.

"You saw him again, didn't you?" Ginny persisted, her dark brown eyes piercing Margaret's.

"Yes," Margaret said. "I'll tell you the whole story. But later." She checked the tape recorder as the audience rose to its feet. The conductor made his way to the stage and lifted his arms. Margaret pressed "play" and "record" together and as the concert was starting, Ginny leaned over to Margaret.

"I'll hold you to that ... I want to hear the *whole* story," she whispered, then they both turned their attention to the children on stage.

Margaret smiled. There were parts of what happened she longed so share with Ginny; but some would have to remain a secret. For now, anyway.

After the rousing Christmas concert, with Susan appropriately congratulated and settled in Ginny Ashwell's car, Margaret headed out of the school parking lot towards her car. She got in and started the engine, then saw Jason had pulled up beside her. He stopped rolled down his window, giving his mother a wolf-whistle. "Wow, Mom. I saw you walking out. You look like a movie star!"

Margaret grinned from ear to ear that her son noticed. She was, for a change, wonderfully confident. She'd taken time to really pamper herself getting ready for tonight. She'd been to the hairdresser, had a manicure and pedicure, and luxuriated in a bath of lavender-scented sea and Epsom salts. The new silk dress she bought while shopping with her mother fit perfectly, the loosely scooped neck sweeping down across the front, and the skirt falling seductively over her hips. The cobalt blue set off her dark hair perfectly. She looked radiant.

She blew him a kiss. "Thanks, Jason! Good concert, wasn't it? How do you think your sister did?"

"Pretty good for middle school," he commented. "In fact, I didn't know she could play that well. Her solo was awesome. Hey, I'm headed out to Mike's."

"I'll be home before your father is, no doubt, so you be sure to be home at a reasonable hour." Margaret waved affectionately and they drove off in their separate directions.

* * * * * * * * *

Jerry's office building was dressed for the season, with colorful lights blinking around each window. The bare branches of deciduous trees twinkled with white lights as they reached toward heaven, and a lone evergreen in front, attractively decorated with peanut butter stuffed pinecones to feed the birds, twinkled in strands of large, old fashioned multi-colored lights. Margaret parked as close to the door as possible, pulled her sable wrap tightly around her shoulders and headed to the front door, thanking God that the wind wasn't blowing. She did not want her hair to blow around.

She could hear the party before she got close. Already in full swing, everyone would be well plied with alcohol. When she entered the room, she tried to locate Jerry, but could not in the large crowd.

For a moment, she stood in the doorway wondering what to do with her wrap.

"Margaret Ammons, I believe," came a laughing voice behind her. It was Molly Shannon, Jerry's long-time secretary, who was standing with a group of staff members. Before Margaret could respond, Jerry was at her side.

"Molly, take Margaret's coat and put it in my office, will you?" Jerry handed the woman the wrap then put his arm back around his wife's waist. Then as if seeing her for the first time, his eyes widened, "My God, you look absolutely gorgeous!" Jerry stood back and gave her the once-over. Margaret felt almost shy to have him eyeing her that way. Then Jerry glanced past his wife and greeted someone behind her. "Oh, Margaret," he said, slipping his arm possessively around her. "This is a man whose name I'm sure you'll recognized..."

She whirled around and came face to face with Ron Crenshaw's roommate, Joe. Stunned, she only stared at him. He too seemed taken aback.

"Sweetheart," Jerry went on. "This is my long-time business associate J.D. Harkins. J.D., my lovely wife, Margaret."

"Margaret Ammons, of course," J.D. said, taking her hand graciously as he stared into her deep green eyes. She shook his hand and released it quickly.

"Nice to meet you," she managed, averting her eyes.

"Let's all go to the bar and get a drink," Jerry suggested. On spaghetti legs, Margaret allowed herself to be led away from the awkward situation.

Jerry handed Margaret a Scotch and water. "I'm going to leave you two for a moment," he said already walking away. "I see a guy I've got to collect a debt from."

Margaret steadied herself against the bar and sipped her drink, not knowing what to say.

"You're as surprised as I am, I can tell," J.D. Harkins said.

"Well, yes." Margaret didn't like the feeling creeping over her. "I mean, I certainly had heard often enough about you... through Jerry. But I never put together that you were—"

"Ron's roommate, Joe?"

"Yes," Margaret smiled sweetly, belying her desire to flee.

"Well, don't feel too badly. Somewhere in the deep recesses of my mind I knew ol' Jer's wife was named Margaret, but I hardly suspected when I met you at the house that it was you."

She didn't know how to respond, so she stood awkwardly, her face hot with embarrassment. Jerry knew Joe, she thought, panic rising in her throat. So Joe was J.D.! How did she not put the two together? Did Ron not mention Joe's last name, or was she so wrapped up in her own thoughts that she just didn't make the connection? How much had Ron told Joe about their relationship? She could hardly bear the possible ramifications of all of this. She felt nauseated.

"Are you all right?" Jerry asked, suddenly appearing again. He again slipped a protective arm around her as she swooned slightly. "Are you tired? This is a late night for you," his voice was uncharacteristically concerned.

She took a deep breath. "Exactly," she responded, avoiding Joe's eyes. "Really tired, but I'll be fine."

"Good," Jerry patted her arm. "I have to circulate. If you need me, just tell one of the staff and they'll find me." Jerry disappeared into what seemed to be a growing crowd.

Margaret felt better after downing a scotch and soda. But when she turned to survey the gathering, she found herself staring once again at Joe Harkins. She drew in a deep breath and, fortified by the scotch, met Joe's disconcerting gaze.

"Joe, I just never suspected you were J.D., Jerry's business partner."

"We have something in common then. I never suspected when I met you at my house that you were Jerry's wife," he managed a smile, but it was not a friendly smile. "So you came out to visit because you and Ron were family friends."

Margaret felt her guard go up. "I grew up with him."

"Oh, yes. The neighbor."

"The Crenshaws were already in the neighborhood when we moved in."

Margaret was extremely uncomfortable. There was more on Joe Harkins' mind than he had expressed so far, she was sure. It had never occurred to her that her two worlds would ever meet, let alone be entwined in this bizarre way. She had to get away from him. "Excuse me," she said, smiling sweetly. "I see some old friends over there. Nice to see you again, Joe."

Across the room Margaret saw several of the office people she'd known for years, among them two of her favorite long-time friends, Tom and Molly Shannon. They had begun working with Jerry years before when he was just getting started. Jerry always incorporated them into his personal staff whenever he moved up in the business world. They were the glue that kept the day-to-day operations of the company going, while Jerry did the shoulder rubbing. Childless, they were officially dubbed aunt and uncle to Brent, Jason and Susan.

As Margaret approached, Tom raised his eyebrows and did a low wolf-whistle. "You look exceptionally lovely this evening, Mrs. Ammons! Been drinking at the fountain of youth?"

Molly cleared her throat in mock offense, then laughed and hugged Margaret. "I'd say I'd have to agree with him! You look fantastic. It's been so long since the last time we saw you. Where've you been keeping yourself?" Molly asked.

"Kid stuff, mostly," Margaret proffered as an excuse. "In fact, I'm late getting here tonight because of a concert Susan had at the middle school. She had a solo and did a wonderful job. I taped it for Jerry." As she said his name, she looked to see where he might be in this crowd. He was standing at the bar, arm around Abigail. Molly's gaze followed Margaret's.

"Pay no attention to that," she said. "He even puts his arm around me when I'm standing next to him. It's part of the Jerry persona," Molly gave an unconvincing laugh.

This was why Margaret tried to miss office parties and other such get-togethers in recent years; why she didn't visit Jerry at the office any more. She could accept Jerry's flirting from time to time because it was his style, but in recent years it had become more than that. Her gut told her he was unfaithful; she chose not to think about it. She pondered the word "unfaithful" and realized with a start that it applied to her. Yet, in an odd way, she felt what transpired between her and Ron had no connection to her marriage at all. Perhaps that was how Jerry felt. It hurt her that all these years he'd been able to set her aside to attain his goals. She loved Jerry; not in the passionate way she'd loved Ron, but it was a deeply committed love. Nevertheless, after twenty years and three children, Jerry was embedded in her heart and soul.

Molly again tried to make light of Jerry's clinging to Abigail. "You know, Charles has finally gotten used to their playing around. Don't pay any attention to that. It doesn't mean a thing, believe me."

Margaret shook her head. "I know, Molly. It's all right." She excused herself and went into the restroom where she took several deep breaths. *What an irrational reaction after what you've done*, she scolded herself angrily. *You're nothing but a dog-in-the-manger, a hypocrite.*

She went from berating herself to giving herself a pep talk. "You and Jerry have an open marriage, " she said aloud. "So live with it." She replaced her lipstick and smiled into the mirror, then became self-conscious. Determined not to let that part of her personality show, she stood straight. *What is that Ginny says to do? Tell yourself how great you are?* she thought as she stared at her reflection. *OK, here goes: Margaret Ammons, you look fantastic*, she mouthed at herself. With that, she walked back to the party.

Abigail and Jerry were nowhere to be seen, but neither were Tom and Molly. J.D. was nearby, talking with a group of people and Margaret slipped past him hoping not to be noticed. "Scotch," she ordered quietly, "on the rocks this time."

J.D. turned at the sound of her voice. "Well, well. We run into each other again," he observed, moving to join her.

"Seems so," she responded coolly, taking a sip of her drink. This man gave her the willies.

"Have you heard from Ron since you've been back?" J.D. asked.

"No," she responded, deliberately meeting his eyes. "I'm sure he's busy."

J.D. nodded and Margaret noted he seemed slightly off-put by her newfound confidence, but he hesitated only a second. "How much do you know about Ron's life these days?"

"Probably not much," Margaret commented suspiciously. "We didn't have much time to spend catching up." She hoped she appeared casual.

"Frankly, I'm worried about him," J.D. said, studying her for a reaction. "He's not been himself lately."

"Do you mean he is sick?" Margaret asked and thought she made the question sound innocent enough.

"Not in the way you're thinking." J.D. glanced around the room. "Would you be willing to take a little walk with me?" He touched her elbow as if to escort her out but she resisted, pulling her arm abruptly away.

"Surely we can talk right here," she challenged, trying to hide the fear creeping up her spine in the presence of this strange man who had clutched her arm a little too tightly.

"No, we can't talk here. If you won't go with me now, meet me later in Tom's office. I've got some things to tell you I think you will be very interested to know."

Margaret was curious—more than curious—but she wasn't sure she wanted to know what J.D. had on his mind. Nor did she think she could trust him. "What time later?" she asked.

J.D. glanced at his watch. It was a little after ten. "Ten thirty," he said.

Margaret nodded, then turned and walked quickly away, feeling J.D.'s eyes on her back. When she felt no one would notice, Margaret set her drink down on a corner table and made her way to the kitchenette where she made herself a cup of strong instant coffee. There, alone in the dark, she drank it, clearing her head. Twenty minutes later she had left the party through a rear exit of the building and was standing in the parking lot beside her car, nervously fumbling with her keys to open the lock. Once inside, she locked all the doors and pulled quickly away. There was no way she was going to meet J.D. alone anywhere. She rushed in the door of her house and quickly picked up the telephone. Ever since she'd returned home from visiting her mother, she'd wanted to talk to Ron again; she'd hoped he would call, but she knew he wouldn't take the chance of getting Jerry. They'd discussed corresponding by mail, but that seemed dangerous and Margaret told him not to write her. Now, however, she had to talk to him.

"Ron!" Margaret said in great relief when she heard his voice at the other end of the telephone line. "It's Margaret."

Ron had quite clearly been asleep. "Of course it is," he responded warmly. "You think I wouldn't recognize your voice?"

"I need to talk to you about something important," she said, not wanting to take time for the usual pleasantries. "You won't believe what happened tonight."

"Is this something I need to come to attention for?"

"Ron, don't tease me."

"I'm sorry. You're upset. What's wrong and how can I help?"

"It's Joe," she said. "Your housemate, Joe."

Ron's tone changed. "What about Joe?"

"He was at Jerry's office party tonight. He's J.D. Harkins, Jerry's business partner."

"You didn't know Joe was your husband's business partner?"

"No. I did not." Margaret felt anger rising in her throat. Ron seemed to already know this. "How long have you known?"

"I'm relieved. I thought you knew and…well, never mind what I thought. But I figured it out earlier today. I've never paid much attention to where Joe was going on the various business trips, but when you and I were together, I remember you saying your husband was going to be in Palm Beach… and I knew Joe had a meeting there, too. Then I started thinking about his many trips that took him to Indiana. I tied that in with other things he's said, and took a good look at the schedule he left me of where he'd be during the week. It didn't take long for me to put two and two together. How did you find out?"

"In the worst way possible. I arrived at the party and there he was."

"No doubt he recognized you."

"Oh, he recognized me all right. He made me feel very nervous."

"How so?"

"He kept trying to get me aside to tell me something."

Ron came to attention. "What kind of something?"

"I don't know, Ron. Something he said I should know."

"So what came of that?"

"I left surreptitiously. I didn't tell anyone I was leaving; not even Jerry. I had to call you. He led me to believe you might be ill."

Ron was quiet for a moment and Margaret waited for him to comment. He drew a long breath. "Don't give it another thought. He's strange sometimes. Especially after a few drinks. But I do need to see you—there's so much we didn't talk about…"

A car pulling into the driveway caught her attention and she glanced out the window. Jason was home. Quickly she closed the conversation with Ron and ran into the bathroom and turned on the shower. As she suspected he would, Jason came right to her room. "Mom?" he called through the closed door.

"I'm about to get in the shower," Margaret called back as casually as she could. "Do you need me?"

"No, just wanted you to know I'm home. Where's Susan?"

"She's spending the night out."

"Want some hot chocolate? I'm going to make some," Jason offered.

"Sounds great," Margaret said, and her heart warmed at her son's thoughtfulness.

Chapter 14

When the telephone rang the next morning Margaret realized the sun was pouring into her room and her head was pounding. She fumbled for the receiver keeping her face buried in the pillow. "'lo?" She muttered.

"Margaret? Is that you?" It was Ginny Ashwell.

Margaret sat up slowly and blinked her eyes. "Yes, it's me." She looked around the room and noticed Jerry had not come home.

"Did I wake you?" Ginny asked.

"No, not really."

"Yes, I did. What's wrong? You sound terrible."

"Too much partying," Margaret responded.

"That's not like you," Ginny said, then quickly came to the point. "Want to meet me for lunch? I've got a business proposition for you."

Margaret knew what the proposition was; Ginny had been asking her to work with her in her children's clothing store for some time. Ginny had commented several times recently how the business had grown since the county was becoming so affluent and she needed help. Well, Margaret thought, a change of scenery and a chance to talk to her old friend would be good. She arranged to meet her at a coffee shop along the White River.

The two women ordered salads and made small talk. It was the first time they'd been together without the children for some time. As the waiter was clearing their dishes, Margaret surprised Ginny.

"I'm resigning as PTO president," she announced.
"Now why in the world would you want to do that?"
"It's someone else's turn," Margaret said bluntly. "Maybe yours."
Ginny laughed and shook her head. "Not mine, I don't have time to turn around as it is. And that's exactly why I wanted to talk to you. Like I told you on the phone, I have a proposition for you," Ginny grinned. "I want you to come work for me in my shop. And before you say no again, consider this. I'd like you to buy into it; we could be partners."

Ginny tailored for children, making clothing to order as well as purchasing special items from fashion centers around the world. It was an exclusive shop, catering to mostly upper-income clientele, and Ginny was ready to expand. "You can help me," she said. "If you will."

It wasn't the first time the two had considered being business partners, but Margaret always had one excuse or another as to why she wouldn't be able to do it. This time Margaret didn't immediately dismiss the idea. "You know, I'm going to think seriously about that," she said, feeling a glimmer of excitement.

"Now, that's out of the way," Ginny said mischievously. "So tell me all about Ron Crenshaw."

By Christmas Eve, Margaret was fully in the spirit of the season. It helped to have her son Brent home. She and the children spent hours decorating the tree, sharing hot mulled cider and listening to Christmas carols on the old stereo from Margaret's youth. They telephoned Margaret's mother and sister to wish them Merry Christmas and considered opening one gift apiece. Jerry came in unexpectedly early just after dark and was highly complimentary of their decorating efforts. The five of them spent the entire evening in the darkened living room lit only by the dancing colored tree lights. It was the best family moment Margaret had known in years. Guilt threatened to rob her of it if she didn't put it out of her mind, so she went to the kitchen and poured herself a drink.

"Want a drink, Jerry?" she called from the kitchen.

"Yep," he called back as he shook one of the packages under the tree, examining it like a child. "No matter how old I get," he told the children. "I still get curious about nicely wrapped packages!"

"I know that," Jason muttered under his breath. His father's penchant for younger women had not escaped him. "Especially young packages."

Jason's snide remark was not lost on Jerry, who gave his son a sideways glance and considered a confrontation, but it was too nice an evening. Besides, it was the truth of the statement, he realized, that made him angry. It startled him though, that the words came from Jason. How, he wondered, and what did his son know. Nothing, really, Jerry convinced himself, for there was nothing to know. Jason would be a married man one day and come to understand things, just as Jerry had come to understand his own father's ways.

Jerry leaned back in his easy chair and watched his family as they opened one package each, a gift sent by their Grandmother Wood. He listened while they talked among themselves, sharing plans for the rest of the time off from school. Brent talked about his girl friend, Jason excitedly related details of the holiday basketball tournament he'd be playing in the weekend after New Year's, and Susan giggled with pleasure at the idea of spending her first New Year's Eve with friends—a girl's sleepover at her best friend's house. Jerry contemplated how naturally Margaret related with the children and how lovely she looked in the light of the Christmas tree. Thinking back to the office party, he felt proud of her. She looked wonderful and had a confidence he hadn't seen in her in years...maybe ever. Now she glowed as she and the children talked and laughed in this beautiful Christmas scene set before him. And he was painfully aware of the fact that he felt a bit on the outside. He'd change that, he thought. He'd always been able to change whatever in his job wasn't working. He did that by attacking the problem head on. The same tactic would no doubt work in his family.

"Doesn't your mother look wonderful tonight?" he asked no one in particular, as he went over to her and gave her a kiss on the forehead. The children just stared in surprise.

"Thank you, Jerry," Margaret said, and quickly blinked tears from her eyes. It was a picture-perfect evening, she thought. The kind of "Father-Knows-Best" type of scene, where no matter the problem, all was solved in thirty minutes.

Chapter 15

For Margaret, working in Ginny's shop proved to be cathartic; a way to relegate Ron to the background again, which is where she knew he had to remain. Jerry, who had never been stingy when it came to material things Margaret wanted or needed, had put up enough money to make Margaret a full partner with Ginny in the business. He had been only too glad to give his wife the money he had won from Michael Goodrich betting on the Redskins/Cowboys game. Michael had phoned Jerry after their agreement to accept $1,000, win or lose and talked him into the $1,000 a point deal he'd wanted originally. It had caused Jerry many a sleepless night, but he'd won. The Redskins beat the Cowboys by 21 points. Jerry was only too happy to pass the money on to his wife thereby easing his relationship with the losing Goodrich, who was surprisingly jovial about his loss. Probably, Jerry reasoned, because Jerry had said the money would go to his wife. It was a ploy he'd used many times before because he knew it sounded good to his clients.

At first, It was hard learning a new life...still trying to have breakfast ready for the kids before school and the house in order before she left for work. The first week she tried to have dinner either set to cook in the oven or cooking all day in the crock pot so that it would be ready when she got home from work, but it became too much to coordinate. It was easier to grab something to eat out, especially when one of the kids had an after school activity. Those evenings she didn't go home at all, but rendezvoused with the child who wasn't involved, ate a quick meal, then went directly to the school, where the activity was taking place. When it involved Jason, sometimes that school was many miles away, and an exhausted Margaret would crawl into bed afterwards wondering why she was doing all this.

But the truth was, Margaret blossomed in her work. It felt good to use skills that had never before surfaced. For years, Ginny had been trying to get her to come into the business, having a great deal more confidence in Margaret's abilities than Margaret herself had. With Margaret's natural organizational skills and surprising advertising prowess, Ginny found more time to work on the creative end. She needed to draw customers from nearby states like Ohio, Illinois, Kentucky as well as expand her small word-of-mouth mail order business.

Since Ginny could leave Margaret in charge of the shop, she had been able to focus on making customer contacts. Business boomed. People seemed to love the idea of a shop that catered to the specific clothing needs of children, had quality merchandise that could be personally tailored to fit their children regardless of size or shape. People came from far and wide.

Ginny soon had to hire more staff to do the tailoring and knitting of special outfits. She searched for women who were competent seamstresses with their own equipment, so they could work in their homes and not have to leave their children home alone or hire sitters.

The work kept Margaret very busy and quelled her constant desire to pick up the phone and telephone Ron. Twice in the three ensuing months since their magical night at the Country Inn, he had written her brief, friendly letters the kind she could leave out on the coffee table for anyone to read. Margaret had responded once, then decided she was playing a silly schoolgirl game and needed to set the past where it belonged...in the past.

Ginny didn't seem to agree, telling her that love was love and not something you could turn on and off. She told Margaret point blank that Ron would always, no matter what, occupy a special place in her heart and she just needed to get used to that. Margaret supposed that was true, but she still didn't write to Ron again. As time passed, it was enough just to hold the memory close and remember fondly from time to time.

One sunny afternoon, as Ginny and Margaret were preparing to close the shop for lunch, the mail arrived. As usual on Monday, there was a large bag. "Let's skip it until later," Ginny suggested. Her stomach had been growling since ten a.m.

"If you want; but maybe we ought to quickly sort the orders so the girls can handle that when they first get in this afternoon."

Ginny relented and stood at the desk quickly sorting the mail, handing to Margaret anything that wasn't an order. Margaret began setting the mail in neat piles to handle later when she saw handwriting she recognized. It was a letter from Ron.

"What is it?" Ginny asked, hearing her friend gasp.

"It's from Ron."

"Why did he write you here?"

Margaret shrugged. "Who knows?"

"You're frowning," Ginny observed.

"Sorry," Margaret said looking up from the letter. "I just skimmed it and didn't understand something." She turned the handwritten letter back to the first page and reread:

"My dearest Margaret: There has been something on my mind from the minute I first saw you again, and I can no longer put off telling you for fear you'll learn it elsewhere. Telling you is the hardest thing I've ever done, and I can only pray you won't hate me. To put it as delicately as possible let me phrase it this way: I have not met your partner, Jerry, but you have met mine. Joe and I have been together for about ten years. You must believe me when I say that this has nothing to do with my love for you, which is real and abiding. I truly believe one day our respective partners will be gone and you and I will be together."

Margaret fell backwards into the desk chair.

"My God, Margaret," Ginny exclaimed, running to her friend. "What's wrong?"

Margaret handed the letter to Ginny. "Tell me he's not saying what I think he is."

Ginny scanned the page, raising her eyebrows only once. "He's gay," Ginny answered in her usual blunt way.

"He can't be gay, Ginny!" Margaret screamed. "He was married; he has a child. He and I were—" Margaret stopped abruptly.

"Lovers?" Ginny finished the sentence.

Margaret threw her hands over her mouth, wanting to deny it as much to herself as to Ginny. "Well, yes."

"OK, so he's been living the gay lifestyle. Maybe it was an escape for him. But he loves you—and you love him."

"No." Margaret protested. "No, Ginny. Oh, my God; oh God! " Margaret stood and steadied herself by holding onto the back of the chair. She retrieved the letter from Ginny's hands and stared blankly at it for it a long moment. Then angrily she crumpled the papers and dropped them into the trashcan. Ron's revelation was beyond her. Like a piece of bad food, the news wouldn't digest. Ginny tried to comfort her friend, but Margaret couldn't see or hear anything but Ron's words, which were burned into her brain.

"Come on, Honey," Ginny urged, slipping her arm around her friend's shoulders. "Let's go."

They drove together in silence along the river to a little run-down looking restaurant that belied the delicious and low-priced cuisine. It was a favorite place of the locals, who held it as a closely guarded secret.

"Ginny," Margaret said before they got out of the car. "You're like a sister to me and I'm frightened. I need to tell you something, especially now after what I just learned about Ron…"

"You slept with him when you were in Washington."

Margaret's eyes widened.

"Don't be so chagrinned. You know, Margaret, you've not had an easy time of it. For once in your life, you dared to dream. I think that's good."

"I did more than dream, Ginny," Margaret's voice was almost a whisper. "I couldn't help myself. Nothing seemed real. I felt like I did when I was nineteen. I couldn't make myself believe I was forty years old and he was forty-four…that we had completely separate lives for all those years. It was as though we'd never been apart. I ignored everything rational. When I was with him, the person I am now was just an observer in the drama that was being played out around me. Somehow I was not in this body; I was in Margaret Wood's body twenty years ago. I was young, beautiful, in the middle of the most exciting time of my life and able, because of the benefit of going back in time, to really enjoy what people who are truly that young cannot. I could appreciate how that special love we shared secretly for so long was something that doesn't happen very often.

"And somehow, it had nothing to do with who I am…it was all about finishing a chapter in a book that I had put down twenty years ago…" She took a deep breath and gave a short laugh. "Twenty years, Ginny. Twenty years that dissolved in one precious moment."

Ginny had been staring intently as Margaret spoke, hanging onto every word. "That you were in love was clear from the moment you got back," she said. "I was just afraid Jerry would notice." She opened the car door, then leaned back toward her friend. "And did you finish that chapter in that book, Margaret?"

Slowly, very slowly, Margaret shook her head. "I can't stand it, Ginny. He's on my mind all day, and then when I go to bed at night, I feel him next to me…I want to be with him…if I had thought making love to him would close the chapter, I was wrong. It just left more questions. These past few months working with you have helped so much, but he's always there on my mind. Even now…even now that I know he's gay." Tears threatened and she grabbed a Kleenex.

"Does Jerry suspect anything at all?"

"No."

"How do you know?"

"He's so busy with his job—his friends…"

"You're sure he can't tell there's something different, Margaret, because there is something different about you."

Margaret blew her nose, then shook her head. "He really doesn't notice me that much."

Ginny reached over and patted Margaret's hand. "Let's go eat."

Chapter 16

It was an unusually hot May afternoon at the ball field. Parents were sitting on bleachers, in lawn chairs, on blankets, and some were milling around talking. Small children toddled after larger ones, carrying hot dogs and lollipops, drinks in cans and baby bottles. The air was still and the sun beat down on the hot, dusty ballplayers.

"All right, Jason," Margaret cheered as her son came up to bat. She stretched her legs out in front of her hoping to get a little browner. It seemed attending baseball games was her only way of getting a tan these days, and she loved the feeling of the hot sun against her skin. She sat with a crowd of faithful parents supportive of their baseball-playing sons. For Margaret, the sports season never ended, at least not since Jason had been about eight years old. In the fall, it was soccer; in winter, basketball; in the spring, baseball. By now Margaret was used to it. And she'd become something of an expert in dressing for games. She knew that for the first baseball games, she needed to bring a chair, sweater and raincoat, then for later ones, a chair, bug spray and suntan lotion, wearing as little clothing as was presentable in public. The weather changed that much in just a few weeks.

"Strike!" called the umpire, adjusting his hat and getting back down in position as the ball whizzed past Jason's knees.

"Ah, that was low!" Margaret called out. "Come on, Jason, ignore the ump. Hit that ball. You can do it!"

Jason got in position, bat high, eyes riveted on the pitcher. Other parents were cheering for him; too, knowing Jason could knock the ball out of the park if he hit it squarely. Margaret noticed jealously how many fathers attended these games...but Jerry rarely was able to. He was almost always out of town. And football was his game. One of Jerry's biggest disappointments was that neither of his sons cared as much as he did about "the game."

The pitcher wound up and threw the ball. The bat made contact, but it flew up over the backstop. Twice more the ball went foul. Crowd intensity increased. Margaret was erect in her seat now, crossing her fingers. The crowd was calling Jason's name loudly; the pitcher, who seemed like a man rather than a high school boy, eyed the catcher, shook his head, then nodded. He wound up again, glanced at the bases, then let the ball fly. There was the crack of the bat, and this time the ball flew high into the air over second base.

"Go, Jason, go!" Margaret shouted, jumping up and down.

With great expectation she watched the ball soar as the outfield backed up, running toward where they expected it to land. The outfielder's glove reached up; Jason was making it to second, the runner at third was holding. The ball began to fall; all eyes were on it. Suddenly as the outfielder continued to back up he stumbled and the ball landed with a thud about a foot behind him. The boy at third base took off, and Jason rounded second. The third base coach was signaling him to go on, and he did, the ball—close on his heels—landed at the cut-off man, was thrown toward the catcher...but Jason was there, sliding into home, to the roar of his teammates and the crowd. Margaret had tears of pride in her eyes as she watched her beaming son being congratulated by all the other players and his coach.

The game lasted another two hours. Jason's run had tied the game, and it went into additional innings. Margaret had caught a lot of sun by the time she and Jason headed home.

"You did a great job!" Margaret exclaimed, giving him a little hug as they walked toward the car.

"I blew it in the field."

"No, you didn't. Only one ball got away."

Jason shrugged. "I'm gonna take a shower then go to Mike's

house…he wants to go to a movie. I'll probably just spend the night."

Mike and Jason had been friends since fourth grade. It seemed from that time on one was always at the other's house. It was a tradition in the summer that they spent a week at a time at the other's house at least once. Margaret smiled, thinking of the boys as children, wondering now if their friendship would extend beyond high school.

As soon as he got home, Jason dropped his dirty uniform in the laundry room and headed to the bathroom. The phone rang. Margaret grabbed it as she poured herself a glass of iced tea.

"Hey, Sweetheart!" It was Jerry calling from his hotel room, and from the way he was talking, it sounded as if the meeting was going his way. Sometimes it seemed he and Margaret had their best relationship on the telephone. "Whatcha up to?" he inquired with real interest.

"Jason and I just got back from his game."

"Great. How'd he do?"

"You should have been there to see him, Jerry. He did so wonderfully…he got the most exciting home run—a double."

"I know, I know. I hate that I always have to be away…tell me more about it."

Margaret related the details proudly; deep down hoping to make Jerry really sorry he hadn't been there. Jason never asked any more why Daddy wasn't there like he used to when he was little, but she could see it in his eyes sometimes.

"When's his next game?"

"High school or rec league?"

"He's playing both!"

"He always plays both."

"Well, when's either next game?"

Margaret stretched the phone cord to the refrigerator where the schedule hung. "His last school game is Monday night. The rec league goes on another two weeks, and those games are Saturdays."

"I'll be home Monday. Can we have a date and go to his game?"

"You must have hit the jackpot there in San Francisco. Wow! A real date!" Margaret teased. "I haven't heard you sound this 'up' for years." She was excited about the possibility of Jerry showing up for Jason's last school game of his junior year.

"We're doing real well. You remember J.D. Harkins—you met him at the Christmas party. He's been working with me on this for over a year and with his help, we've made a deal with Ralph Simpson you wouldn't believe. All of a sudden he and Ralph got along like a house on fire and we sealed the deal over dinner. I haven't seen them since."

Thoughts of J.D. Harkins—Joe—made Margaret sick. She prayed Jerry would never again have to deal with that man.

"How's my baby girl?" Jerry went on.

"Susan's fine. She's practicing for the big musical production."

"When's that?"

"End of the month."

"I'm going to do everything I can to be there. I'm thinking about taking some time off right after the kids get out of school, so we can go somewhere as a family."

"Right," Margaret responded guardedly. Jerry hadn't been this exuberant since he first got into public relations, but she knew he was full of well-intended talk that often didn't come to fruition. And she hated it when his guilt made him make promises both of them knew he wouldn't keep.

A beautiful Saturday stretched before her. She wandered down to the river that ran long the woods a few hundred feet behind their house. There people were fishing along the gently sloping grassy banks. She walked about a mile down the river listening to the birds singing and inhaling the wonderful fragrances of viburnum and wild honeysuckle. It took her about an hour to make a complete circle through the woods and back to her house. Ginny was pulling in her driveway just as Margaret walked up.

"Got time for iced tea and a chat?" Ginny called out her car window.

"Of course. Come on in." Margaret pulled out a handful of mail, plopped it on the kitchen table and got out two glasses for the tea.

"One ice cube," Ginny instructed as she always did, despite the fact that they'd been drinking tea together for years. As Ginny stirred sweetener into her tea, Margaret glanced at the mail, eyes falling on familiar handwriting. Quickly she snatched up and opened the letter. Ginny gave a knowing smile. "Ron?"

Margaret nodded, opening the envelope with shaking hands. "I wonder why he sent it here instead of the shop?"

"Maybe he likes to live dangerously!" Ginny's brown eyes twinkled.

Margaret's eyes raced over the page. "Oh, my God!" she gasped. "Ron's here. Here in Indianapolis. And he wants to see me."

Chapter 17

Ron's letter said he would be staying about fifty miles out of town at the Somersby Tavern, and begged Margaret to meet him there Friday evening. He said he would be waiting; she didn't have to contact him. She wrestled with the idea up to the moment when she would have to get ready if she were going. Ginny's advice was go; that it could do no harm and obviously thought it was all so very romantic, and that kept the flame aglow in Margaret, who was sure it wasn't a good idea to be alone again with Ron. The bond between them was too strong, in spite of everything else. Margaret could not accept the lifestyle of Ron, this stranger who said he was gay. But the Ron who lived in her heart was strong and romantic; the same man she remembered from her youth. She wanted to see him. She wanted him to tell her that what he had told her wasn't true, that it had been some kind of test of her love. True or not, in the months since their reunion, Margaret had determined to put any feelings she had for him aside. Nothing could come of a relationship with him, even if he didn't profess to be gay. Still she had to go. It was a frightening proposition, but calling or writing him to say it was over just wouldn't do. Not after rejecting him that way once before.

The drive to Somersby seemed endless; busy main roads became single lanes, winding and twisting, canopied by tall, graceful trees. She was glad she'd been to the Tavern once before, or she would have thought she was lost.

The day had been hot and humid, and Margaret was dressed in summer slacks and light blouse. Now she turned the car's air conditioning off and opened a window to let in the cooler evening air. About ten miles from her destination, Margaret began shaking. She felt an overwhelming desire to turn around and go back home; to call the Inn and leave a message—some message that wouldn't hurt Ron like she'd hurt him all those years before. Some message that would convey the idea that she loved him, but their relationship needed to be from afar. Impossible, she said to herself angrily. Facing him is the only way. There was a feeling of foreboding that she couldn't shake; she wanted desperately to avoid whatever lay ahead. If only she could turn back the clock and put Ron back as a wonderful, romantic memory.

She thought of Ginny's question, "What do you have to lose by going?" and Margaret realized with a start that she had everything to lose.

It worried her to think that once she saw Ron again, she might not be able to resist falling into his arms. It was a feeling she could not understand in light of his confession, but it was the truth. She could not equate the love she felt for him with the complicated truth that he preferred relationships with men.

As she drew into the small town, the streetlights were bright enough for her to see her face in the rear view mirror. She glanced at herself quickly, hoping she looked confident. She did not. Suddenly Somersby Tavern came into view—an old, sandstone building, part of which had been an original tavern over a hundred years before. Some said it was haunted. Ginny fully believed it was, but then Ginny believed her own house was haunted. Margaret was skeptical about ghosts in general, but she had to admit the tavern had a certain aura, accentuated by the drawings depicting scenes of the ill-fated lovers who legend had it lost their lives there back in the days when men took the law into their own hands.

Before she stopped the car she saw Ron standing strong and confident in the entranceway. The sight of him melted her heart, once again all reality fading as she felt his chemistry seeking hers. He was opening her car door and embracing her before she could think. "Thank you for coming," he whispered in a scene reminiscent of their reunion at his mother's funeral. Then he quickly drew back and without a word, took her arm and led her inside. He directed her through the dining room, up the stairs and directly to one of the guestrooms. Margaret was alarmed. He seemed so tense; his look was strange.

"Thank God you came," he whispered, closing the door. And once again he took her in his arms.

"Ron, I didn't come to be with you—in your room." Margaret was adamant and she stepped away from him.

"All right, Margaret. I know that. If you think I brought you here simply to throw you into bed, you're wrong. But we can't talk like we need to in a public place. And we have to talk. I've been dying by inches since my last letter. And you never responded..."

Margaret was embarrassed. "What was there to say, Ron? I mean—well, what was there to say?"

They stood awkwardly looking at each other. Margaret thought Ron looked good and was surprised, thinking he ought to look remorseful or weak or something other than strong, attractive and confident. "Come over here," he said, offering her a chair by the window. "Would you like a drink?" He bent down to the small guest refrigerator. "We have all kinds of nearly-frozen bottles of scotch, bourbon, wine and...let me see, gin and vodka."

"Scotch," Margaret said, pushing her chair closer to the table. Ron took out two bottles of Scotch, opened them and poured a glass for each of them. "Want me to order dinner?"

"No," Margaret responded, perhaps too emphatically. "Unless you think we're going to be here that long," she added self-consciously.

Ron smiled at her, a haunting, disturbing smile. "Cheers," he said flatly, offering her the drink.

Margaret didn't comment, but accepted the glass and drank deeply, giving away her nervousness. The burning sensation of the scotch seeping down her throat was welcome; soon, she hoped, she would feel more relaxed and able to listen calmly to whatever Ron had to say. For now, her heart was in her throat.

EVEN NOW

They sat awhile staring out the window at the front gardens of Somersby Tavern, which were beautifully manicured. Trees still wore their spring blossoms. Iris bloomed in profusion and climbing roses were budding against their trellises.

"I can't stand your silence," Ron exclaimed, pushing hard away from the table and getting up to pace the room. "You've got to say something. Get mad. Shout. Cry. But we have to start this conversation somewhere." He turned and looked at her expectantly.

"I don't know what you want me to say," Margaret retorted in obvious distress.

"You're right; you're right. I'm the one who has something to say. I'm just having trouble getting started. This is so damn hard. It took me years of therapy to be convinced I was OK; that I'd found my 'true' self. And then you come along and I suddenly am lost in confusion again. I still don't understand; maybe never will. But I'm not ashamed, Margaret. I'm no pervert. I feel just as I always have; love what I always loved. I bleed if I'm cut, and I heal and go on. I am truly the same person I always was—I desperately want for you to understand that. But you...your lack of response to my letter—that said everything."

Margaret finished her drink quickly. "If it helps, Ron," she said, going over to him. "I'm as confused as you are. Probably more so." She quickly moved back away from him and asked for another drink; being too close to him aroused emotions she thought his secret lifestyle had managed to squelch.

Ron poured a second drink for them both. "How can I help you understand? Is it possible? Or should I just give up and go away?"

He was so sensitive; so sincere. Margaret owed it to the old friend who stood before her to hear him out. "Just begin at the beginning," she said, taking a pillow from the bed and propping it comfortably behind her in the chair.

With that, he seemed to calm down. "Well," he said, sitting across from her at the round wooden table. "It really all begins with your letter, twenty years ago. You'd married Jerry. I knew it way my fault, but I never thought I was the man for you; not good enough," he held up his hand to stop her protest. "In an odd way, I was relieved to get your "Dear John" letter. But I was also devastated. My parents, especially my mother who was so insightful, were really worried. She suggested therapy. I knew Alice then; she worked in a cubical next to mine. She recommended a woman therapist she'd gone to college with. Eventually I got into a group therapy program and met Joe.

Margaret put up her hand. "I don't want to know anything about Joe."

Ron stared at her, then nodded. "To shorten this long, sick saga, the therapist and the group managed to convince me that my marriage troubles and losing you were because I was homosexual. In my state of mind, what she said made sense. I started back with my therapist—I've seen her a few times throughout the years; and told her about you. I don't think she's had much experience with this kind of thing, but she said something that made sense. She said I should try living alone for a while; not have any contact with old friends to try to sort things out without influence. Before I did that, I wanted to give us a chance—hoping against hope that you'd say you'd run off with me to Tahiti or some such place...

"But, of course you wouldn't," Ron said ruefully. "I knew that. You've got it all—why should you? Anyway, I've taken the first step. Actually I've taken two steps. Talking to you was really the second step. The first step was, well, I left Joe."

"Oh, for Pete's sake, Ron," Margaret spat out, the anger she felt over that situation at last surfacing. "I don't want to hear about Joe," she repeated

"All right!" Ron held his hand up in submission. "All right. I'm sorry. Let me put it another way. I've been living in my dad's house for the past few weeks. I sold the other house to, well—to the other tenants. I stored most of my things, and I feel freer than I ever have."

"Are you going to continue to stay with your father?" Margaret inquired.

"Probably not. One thing I was thinking about was making a move out here so I could somehow be part of your life."

"But that doesn't follow your therapist's suggestion."

"Not completely. I'd probably go away first for a while, maybe till next year even. But I thought if I settled around here, we could...be...friends."

Though Margaret had relaxed, she knew what Ron was proposing was out of the question. She remembered that she came here to break it off completely, but Ron's countenance changed suddenly from a confident, hopeful man, to that of a wounded puppy. He looked pleadingly into her eyes. "Margaret, please don't hate me; please say we can be friends again."

Margaret looked incredulously at Ron. "Friends? How can we be just friends?"

"Because we are friends. I know we have a long way to travel to get back to where we were. But we started as friends; childhood friends who came to love each other. There's something between us that you can't deny, Margaret. Neither can I. Whatever it is that holds us together, it's strong. I'm not asking that we jump right back to where I want us to be...just to a level of friendship that allows us to learn about each other; to get to know each other in a way that twenty years has not. For God's sake," Ron shouted. "You know the worst of me, Margaret. Now get to know the best of me."

Margaret finished her drink quickly. She would not be shouted at. Not after the pain this situation had thrust upon her. "OK, Ron. Here's what I think. I can be your friend. But at a distance. Not with you living nearby."

Ron's face fell. "I'm the same person who made love to you at the Country Inn in December; the same person you loved twenty years ago. Sure, there's more baggage now. There would be with anyone. We all carry baggage; it just differs from person to person. But in here," Ron slammed his fist into his chest. "In here, I'm the same Ron Crenshaw. What we had—have—is separate from anything and everything else." He went over and put his hands on her shoulders. "We can be lovers again, Margaret. I know it can't be right now, while your kids are at home; while you're married, but one day..."

"You don't understand Ron. It's not them standing in the way of our relationship. It's you...." She stood up to leave. It was too uncomfortable here alone with him; her emotions too conflicting. She walked swiftly to the door. As she turned, he came close and took her face in his hands. For a long time their eyes locked. Hers searched his for some sign of who she thought he was; his searched hers for some sign of forgiveness. Her heart ached as she felt him explore the depths of her soul. Then he kissed her lips, gently, lovingly, then simply held her close.

Margaret cried, tears cascading down her cheeks. "I should never have come back into your life..." she sobbed. "I've ruined it for you."

"You didn't come back into my life, Margaret, because you never left my life," he whispered. "Deep inside, I knew the day would come when we'd be together again. I've lived for that. It was meant to be. Ours was a chapter that was left without conclusion for twenty years. A book with no ending. We have to create that ending, make it a happily-ever-after ending—you and I, together."

Margaret took a deep breath, closing her eyes tightly to regain control. "Ron, things are as they are; we can't really start over, you know that. And we're not teenagers. It's not like we have time on our side."

"We will be together, even if we're both in wheelchairs."

"I just don't know what to say," Margaret said, shaking her head slowly.

"Say you still love me."

She looked at him for a long time, emotions churning. "I do love you," she said softly. "But our lives have taken entirely different paths. We're two different people now than who we were then."

"What you're really saying is that I'm different." Ron clearly took offense at her words and he sounded angry. "You think being gay is a sin. What about adultery? Are you saying that some sins are worse than others?"

"No!" Margaret protested, but she was at a loss for words. It was true—Ron seemed the same, but the lifestyle he had been living was something she couldn't understand and knew little of. And she certainly couldn't accept that it was possible for him to have loved her all this time and still lived in a relationship with Joe. If he had been living with another woman, it would be a totally different matter. At least, she thought it would. But it made no difference, because that wasn't the reality.

She knew now why her mother had been so secretive about Ron. She knew now what he was talking about when he said there were things he never straightened out with his mother. So many things that were murky before were becoming clearer. But the one thing she could not deny was that the feeling she had for him had not changed. The Ron she knew, or thought she knew, she loved. It would take a long time to straighten that out in her head and heart.

"Tell me, Margaret, that when I move here—whenever that is, that you will see me."

Margaret moved away from him. "Ron, I don't know. You talked about sin and you're right. What we've done is a sin, though you must believe that I always felt when it came to my feelings for you, God would somehow understand. Still, I know clearly from long-ago Sunday school classes that the only way to be forgiven a sin is to change the behavior. If I continue seeing you while I'm married, the behavior hasn't changed. And you—" She began to lose control and reached blindly for the doorknob. "I have to go."

Ron looked desperate. He grabbed both her arms with such force it jarred her purse loose. It fell to the floor, spilling its contents, which scattered everywhere. When she tried to reach for it, he held her tighter. "Don't leave me Margaret. Not now. Not like this."

Margaret stood limply, neither responding nor resisting. His face clouded and, looking totally dejected, he released his grip. "We will be together, Margaret," he said, staring deeply into her eyes. "I just know it. We were meant to be."

Margaret stayed glued to the spot as Ron bent down to pick up the items that belonged in her purse. He kept glancing at her as he put the belongings back inside and tried unsuccessfully to snap the top shut. "Good-bye Margaret," he said finally, eyes glistening.

Chapter 18

Margaret hurried down the steps and through the lobby of Somersby Tavern. She wanted to get out of there as fast as she possibly could. For a moment, she stood confused as to how to get out of the old building, whose downstairs was a maze of small rooms and doors. People stared at her obvious distress. "Where's the door to the street?" she cried to a passing waiter. He pointed and she rushed toward it, only halfway acknowledging someone she saw out of the corner of her eye who spoke to her. She burst through the door and into the parking lot. Twice her keys fell from her hands, but she managed to get the car door opened and throw herself behind the wheel. She started the engine and pulled onto the main road before she allowed herself to fully breathe.

Her confusion was total, but one thing she knew for sure: As long as she thought of Ron as gay, she would never be able to have a relationship with him. Not even if she were single. The problem was that as she shook with sobs, her body permeated with pain, she wanted desperately to have the Ron she had loved all these years hold and comfort her.

At home she washed her face and fell into bed, but sleep would not come. She saw Ron's disappointed expression each time she closed her eyes. Whatever Ron was or thought himself to be, she loved him. She couldn't imagine not loving him. But she had to separate the Ron she loved from the person he'd become. To do that, she would have to relegate him to the recesses of her mind where he had lived for so long. She would always love him, she knew; but never again physically. He had asked her whether she thought some sins were worse than others. *Yes,* she thought grimly. *Some sins are worse than others.*

After tossing and turning for over an hour and finally realizing sleep wasn't going to come, she turned on the radio to try to find something to distract her from her errant thoughts. She maneuvered the luminescent dial until she came to a station that she knew would give her mostly music. Hopefully, music to fall asleep by. Then, finding what she was looking for, she lay back and tried to relax. Time passed; her eyelids got heavy, her mind was wandering aimlessly through many subjects until the music began to remind her of Ron. It was that song; the one he'd sung to her in those happy moments when they danced together at the Country Inn...

"Even now, when I never hear your name and the world has changed so much since you've been gone. Even now I still remember and the feeling's still the same and this pain inside of me goes on and on...Even now..."

It was after midnight. Even though it was nearly June, the house felt cold and lonely. Margaret had been glad at first when she came in that no one was home, but now she longed for the presence of another human being. She picked up a book lying beside her bed. Agatha Christi's *Cards on the Table*. She remembered that Jason had given it to her as a birthday present many months back and she still hadn't read it. Now she opened the pages and tried to focus on the adventures of Hercule Poirot, but though her eyes were reading the words, her mind was not. She soon found she had turned several pages without having the faintest idea what she had read.

With determination, she went back to the beginning and read deliberately trying to focus. *I will put Ron out of my mind,* she thought. That said, she forced herself to concentrate on the pages. She had read the first chapter and was beginning to be interested in the book when the doorbell rang.

Shocked that someone would be at the door at this time of night, she gasped and sat bolt upright. Quickly she turned out the light. Pulse racing, she went to the window and peered into the darkness as she fumbled with her robe and rushed downstairs. It must be Ron. He'd come to tell her it was all a lie, that he had been testing the strength of her love because he'd lost so many times before; that this lie was his defense against being hurt again. With joy, she bounded toward the front door, then stopped suddenly in the entrance hall in the dark. What if it wasn't Ron? She turned on the porch light and could make out two figures through the glazed pattern on her glass door. Pressing her nose to the glass, she could see it was two policemen.

"Yes?" she called through the door nervously.

"Mrs. Ammons?"

Margaret felt a strong sense of foreboding. "Yes," she replied tentatively.

"Police. Could we talk to you?"

Frightened, Margaret asked them to slip their identification through the mail slot in the door. She held it up with shaking hands, but her eyes would not focus. Tentatively she opened the door and returned their I.D.

"I'm Sergeant McClelland from the Indianapolis State Police," the larger man said. "This is Detective Munsey. May we come inside?"

Still shaking, Margaret escorted the two police officers into her living room. "Has something happened to one of my children?" she asked, panic rising in her throat.

"No, ma-am." The officer responded quickly. "Could we all sit down?" Sergeant McClelland asked.

Margaret's mind was beginning to work at a furious pace. "You sure my children are all right? Oh my God—Jerry! What's happened to Jerry?" she asked frantically.

"No, no, Mrs. Ammons," Detective Munsey assured her. "This has nothing to do with your family. We've come strictly to talk to you. We need to ask you where you were around ten o'clock this evening."

Margaret's heart began pounding even harder, wondering why that should be of any concern to the police. "Well," she said uncertainly, glancing at the watch on her wrist as if it could give her some help. "I think I was here reading."

"You think?" the detective frowned. "Could you be more precise?"

"Well..." she stammered again. "I didn't really look at the time when I came in."

"So you were out this evening? Do you mind telling us who with?"

"Friends. Just—friends."

The detective pulled out a notebook. "Could you name these friends for me please."

Margaret hesitated. "I wish you'd tell me what is wrong. You're scaring me. Do you think I've done something wrong?"

"Is there a reason for us to think you've done something wrong, Mrs. Ammons?"

Margaret did not like the direction this was taking. As far as she knew it was not a crime to go into a man's hotel room. Did Jerry have her followed? Maybe these men weren't really police officers. After all, she had given their I.D. only a cursory glance. She stood up and tried to sound formidable. "I have to insist that you tell me what this is all about...or I need to call my attorney."

"You may of course call your attorney if you wish," Sergeant McClelland offered, also standing.

Margaret looked at her watch again. One-fifteen. She sighed. "I really don't want to have to wake anyone at this hour. Can't you please just tell me what this is all about? Surely I have a right to know."

"We're here concerning a Ronald Wesley Crenshaw," Sergeant McClelland said after glancing over at the detective for approval. "Do you by chance know Mr. Crenshaw?"

Margaret flushed so vividly that she could not have denied knowing him even if she had wanted to.

"Yes," she answered weakly. "Why do you ask?"

"Are you aware that Mr. Crenshaw was staying tonight at the Somersby Tavern in Hartfield?"

Margaret tried to sound calm as she wondered what possible interest in her relationship with Ron the police could have. It had to be something Jerry instigated. And clearly these men already know the answer to their question. She could no longer deny being there.

"Yes, I knew that," she responded quietly, her voice beginning to tremble.

"Were you with him at any time this evening?"

There was a long silence while Margaret tried to figure out what to say. She was afraid to answer and gave serious thought to waking their lawyer even at this hour. But why? Though she couldn't understand why she would need her attorney, she was beginning to feel something was very, very wrong.

She nodded. "Yes, I saw him this evening." Then, looking first from one to the other of the men who had invaded her living room, she added, "Ron and I have been friends since childhood. His mother died recently. He was in town; we were going to have dinner together." She stopped short, hoping she hadn't said too much.

"At Somersby Tavern?"

"That's right."

"Did you go into Mr. Crenshaw's room, Mrs. Ammons."

"Of course not," the words were out of Margaret's mouth before she had time to think. She slumped back down on the couch; again sure the police officers knew she was lying.

"Are you sure?" Sergeant McClelland's voice was all business as he now assumed a somewhat adversarial tone. "We have a witness who says she saw you coming out of the stairway just after 10 tonight."

Margaret hung her head. "I did go to his room," she whispered. Then she stood up angrily. "But what difference does that make to you? Is my husband having me watched?" Even before the sentence was fully out of her mouth, she wished she hadn't said it. "Please, just tell me what this is all about," she added quickly.

"I'm sorry to tell you that your friend Mr. Crenshaw was found shot to death in his room. Would you know anything about that, Mrs. Ammons?"

Margaret sank back onto the couch gasping in disbelief. "No," she cried. "No! How? Why?"

"Was Mr. Crenshaw alive when you left him?"

"Of course he was..." Margaret stared at the two men in front of her, the impact of the situation suddenly weighing heavily upon her. "Oh, my God," she shouted. "I don't believe it! Tell me it isn't so. Tell me this is some kind of cruel joke."

"Is this yours?" Detective Munsey held her address book. It obviously was one of the items that fell from her purse when Ron grabbed her and had not been noticed when he picked things up. With sinking heart, she felt trapped.

"Yes," she whispered.

"We'd like for you to come downtown with us to give us a formal statement."

"Do I have to—tonight, I mean? Am I being arrested?"

"Mrs. Ammons, if you don't go with us of your own free will, I'm afraid we could have to arrest you. You are a key witness in this crime." The detective spoke kindly, but authoritatively. "You may have been the last person to see Mr. Crenshaw alive."

"I don't believe this," Margaret mumbled, but she went obediently to her room and dressed, put on her shoes, brushed her teeth and ran a comb through her hair all of which she did in a trance-like state. The pain in her heart had grown to a severe ache. It was all so unreal. Any moment, she would wake up. She had to.

In the small room where the police had left her to wait alone for her attorney, she paced back and forth, numbed by the events of the past hours. Memories of the Ron she'd known all her life flashed through her mind: the joy that he had been to his parents, to the neighborhood as he delivered the local paper with a smile and his latest joke. As a small boy, Ron was always the one to arrive with a rake in the fall to get up the leaves and a snow shovel in the winter to clear the walks. He always said he was saving the money so he could be a millionaire. And his mother told stories of how he really did save every penny. Everybody knew him.

When he fell in love with her, he had been so patient, so gentle. And twenty years later, he was still the same. Or seemed the same to her. How could he be dead? Why would he be dead?

The door opened and Margaret's attorney, Jack Webster, a distinguished man with salt-and-pepper gray hair and a Boston accent, entered the room and set a briefcase on the table. He looked tired. But, Margaret thought, who wouldn't be tired at three in the morning? He gave her a quick hug.

"Margaret, what's going on here?" his voice was soft and encouraging.

"I don't know, Jack...I just don't know. I was going to have dinner with a friend..."

"The deceased? You were going to have dinner with the deceased?"

Margaret lowered her eyes.

"Margaret," Jack said, lifting her chin. "I'm your attorney and your friend. You've got to be honest with me. I can't help you if I myself don't know exactly what happened."

Margaret dropped her head into her hands, shoulders shaking. "This can't be happening, Jack. It just can't. It's all a nightmare."

"Don't worry," he reassured her. Jack reached across the table and took her hand. "Just start at the beginning so I can get a picture of all this."

"I can't—I can't..." Margaret was getting hysterical. "What difference does it make now anyway? Ron's dead. They think I killed him. Oh, Jack, I'm sorry. I know how this will affect Jerry..."

Jack spent a few moments calming Margaret down, getting her a tissue and a paper cup with water. "Margaret, try to settle yourself. You probably have nothing to worry about; to be honest, they're not sure whether or not Mr. Crenshaw was murdered."

"What!" Margaret said, looking up hopefully. "You mean he's not dead?"

"No, I mean it looks as if he might have shot himself. The gun was found nearby. The police are just troubleshooting right now while detectives investigate the scene."

"Shot himself? What? Ron? Never"

"They didn't tell you that?"

Margaret shook her head angrily. "No. They indicated they thought

I killed him."

"Well, there's some discussion about that. They're investigating still. It doesn't look like a classic suicide apparently. But there are indications he may have had reason to kill himself. His letter to you, his lifestyle."

Margaret looked quizzical. "A letter to me? What letter?"

"Police found a letter in the room addressed to you. It expressed his love for you, stating how he was starting over…maybe he was going to send it to you if you didn't show up tonight." Jack looked concerned. "Margaret, did you know this guy was gay?"

"He said he was gay. We talked about it."

"So what was your relationship here?"

Margaret studied the walls, wiped her eyes again and looked down at the floor. How horrible it felt to have to tell Jack.

"If I'm going to help you, I have to know everything," he said kindly. Jack had been a good friend for many years. He'd helped Jerry in business situations and they had become genuinely good friends. In many ways, Jack reminded Margaret of her father. He had always treated her with the greatest respect, and now she was falling apart before his eyes. She felt shame and anger—at herself and at the world.

"We were in love. I loved him many years ago, before I married Jerry. When we saw each other again last December at his mother's funeral, it all started up again. I'm sorry, Jack, to be such a disappointment, but I did love him."

"So it upset you a lot when you learned he was gay." Jack didn't seem any too happy to realize that there might be a motive for murder.

"Well, of course it upset me…a lot. I didn't understand…well, it doesn't matter. What difference does it make now whether I was upset about it or not?"

Jack shook his head. "Might go to motive," he said. "I'm sure that's what they'll try so say, if it's not ruled suicide."

A policeman appeared at the door and motioned Jack outside. Margaret gulped her water and refilled the cup from the cooler. In seconds Jack was back inside. His face looked grim.

"Margaret, brace yourself. They are about to come in here and charge you with murder. Of course, we'll make bail."

Chapter 19

The always upbeat Ginny Ashwell brought blessed relief to Margaret who was drained mentally and emotionally after the incredible turn of events that had shattered her. Ginny was the first person Margaret called when she got home that morning from the police station and ever-loyal Ginny arrived within minutes. She did not ask any questions as she drove Margaret to an out-of-the-way restaurant where the two could be alone and unrecognized. That in itself was a feat because Ginny was so well known in the community. They sat near the back of the restaurant and Ginny glanced at the menu handed her by a gum-chewing waitress who stood, pad in hand, poised to write down the expected order. While waiting and chewing, the waitress glanced suspiciously at Margaret, who was all but hiding behind the menu, wearing large, dark glasses.

"What do you want to eat?" Ginny asked and Margaret shook her head.

"That's not acceptable," Ginny commented in a motherly way, then went ahead and ordered ham sandwiches and iced tea. She sipped her iced tea, patiently waiting for Margaret to gather her thoughts and begin to talk. The two had faced difficult situations together before; not as intense perhaps as this, but together they'd weathered many storms. Margaret was so exhausted she felt numb, but she was comforted being in the presence of her good friend and grateful for Ginny's ability to assess a situation and respond accordingly. Ginny had a gift of being unobtrusive, yet interested; not possessive, yet protective. While Ginny sipped her tea and filed a fingernail, Margaret, under cover of her dark glasses, absently studied the various patrons as they came and went through the swinging doors to the restaurant. She felt teary, but she was drained of every drop.

When the meal was served, Ginny broke the silence. "Eat," she ordered gently, bringing Margaret back from far away.

"Do the kids know where I am?" Margaret felt disconnected from everyone, even herself, as if she were acting out a dream. The dream somehow didn't include children, but some primal instinct reminded her of that responsibility.

"I left a note on the door that I'd taken you to lunch," Ginny reminded her. "When do you expect them…I can call."

Margaret picked up her fork and in robotic fashion began eating the lettuce and ham, chewing slowly, pondering Ginny's statement. Then she nodded her head, as if things were slowing coming back to her. "Jason probably won't be back until dinner; Mike's family took the boys camping overnight. But Susan might actually be getting home about now."

"Do you want me to call and see if Susan's home?"

"I'd better do it myself," Margaret said, fishing in her purse for a quarter. "I don't want her to think anything is wrong." Though she realized how ridiculous that sounded, she continued looking for the correct change, and the more she looked, the more flustered she became. The contents of her purse were still jumbled from when Ron had accidentally pulled it from her arm.

Ginny reached her hand across the table and laid it upon Margaret's. "Stop. Breathe slowly. Take a drink of tea and get yourself together," she said, handing Margaret a quarter from her own purse. "Keep it short and try to be positive when you talk to Susan. There's time for explanations later."

Margaret didn't have to worry about how she sounded because Susan wasn't home. After the phone rang six times, the answering machine picked up and Margaret left a quick and fairly calm message then went back to her friend and her lunch.

"Where's Jerry? I mean, I'm sure he's out of town, he always is. But where?"

"San Francisco. He's due back today, I think. Or Monday."

"So you haven't tried to reach him?"

Margaret looked up anxiously and Ginny could tell it was the last thing Margaret wanted to do.

"You've been through so much," Ginny said sympathetically. "Did you reach your attorney?"

"He was with me the whole time—well, when I got to the police station I called him," Margaret answered, pushing away her half eaten sandwich. "But it was worse when he came."

"How so?"

Margaret set down her napkin and for the first time removed her sunglasses, revealing red, swollen eyes that were once again brimming with tears. "Ginny, he acted so—how can I say it—condescending. I would have rather just gone ahead and told the police everything that happened...he wouldn't let me say anything."

"Well, Jack was protecting you," Ginny offered.

"It was more than that," Margaret stated flatly.

Ginny frowned. "Sounds like your attorney acted like you were guilty?"

"He made me feel guilty. He acted like I had something to hide."

"What do they think you have to hide?"

"Ginny, they think I killed Ron...they say it wasn't suicide."

"It wasn't suicide?" Ginny shrieked, then realizing that people were looking, she dropped her voice. "Surely something like that is quite—obvious..."

Margaret stifled a sob. "They wouldn't give me any details. All that really matters is Ron is dead. And I might as well have done it," she said, shoulders sagging.

Ginny looked astonished. "What ever would make you say that?"

"The way I treated him...I've abandoned him over and over again." Margaret could hardly bear to think of it. So vivid in her memory were the times throughout their lives when she rejected Ron—how could she ever have expected him to believe she really had loved him? And now there was no chance to even try to convince him. He was dead. Murdered. Talking about it made it seem so real, and she just prayed to wake up and find out she was only dreaming.

* * * * * * * * *

It was evening of the longest day of Margaret's life. Jerry was coming home anytime and she had to tell him everything. There was no getting around it. The thought of it sickened her. And she was so weak and tired, she didn't think it would be possible to get through it.

Jerry was not the understanding kind. Things went smoothly as long as they basically went his way. He had that Latin temperament that caused him to fly off the handle before getting the full story. However, in the case of this story, Margaret knew, there were no parts that wouldn't make him furious. She tried to remember what Jerry actually knew of Ron Crenshaw. As she measured coffee into the filter she forced herself to think back to those tumultuous days when she was dating Jerry but still hoping against hope that Ron would ask her to marry him.

She remembered a balmy evening when she and Jerry walked arm and arm through Georgetown and wandered into a little café where they ordered clams on the half shell and a bottle of wine. It would have been a perfect evening if Margaret's thoughts hadn't kept wandering back to Ron. He had become more distant recently and his mother had more than once made it clear she didn't believe he would ever marry again. It was as if they were conspiring to push her away.

That long ago evening, as she and Jerry finished the clams and were each on their second glass of Chardonnay, Jerry had reached across and taken her hand. "Marry me, Margaret," he had whispered, eyes glistening. Her heart had leapt in her breast and she was so incredibly touched by his deep emotion. "I know I'm not the only one in your life right now," Jerry had continued. "But I want to be." He had continued talking, trying to convince her. As she recollected this scene, she repeated the forgotten words he had said so long ago:

EVEN NOW

"I know I'm not the only one in your life..." What had he known? There in that cozy little café in Georgetown, basking in the warm glow of a good wine and a hopeful lover, she said yes. She told Jerry she would marry him. And then they walked down to the Tidal Basin and made love in the dark under the cherry trees.

Not long afterwards she discovered she was pregnant, and they quickly eloped.

A sudden memory, long lost or pushed back, came to mind. It happened a couple of nights before that fateful evening Jerry proposed. Ron had been home for the weekend and was getting ready to leave town again. They were alone in his father's house, sharing a cigarette after making love. Again Margaret had professed her love for him, and again, though Ron had smiled deeply into her eyes, kissed her, and said simply, "I know." Margaret had gotten angry and left without another word.

The feeling now within her stomach was that of an intense attack of the flu...she had completely wiped out the evening with Ron from her memory. They had been together so many times during that year; had so many quick love-making rendezvous that it hadn't been a particularly memorable scene...but now, in the depth of her depression over his loss, it was clear to her: Ron could very easily be Brent's father. She felt physically ill. Even though her mother had often intimated that, Margaret had always passed it off. She'd never questioned that Brent was Jerry's child. After that first night at the Tidal Basin, they were engaged and made love frequently. Of course Brent was Jerry's child.

Margaret made a pot of coffee and sat down to try to shake off the blanket of depression that enveloped her. If only she could disappear, fade away never to return either to others around her or to herself. She didn't want to exist anymore. She aimlessly began straightening things in the kitchen and gathered up the newspaper Ginny had apparently brought inside when she picked her up earlier in the day. As Margaret unfolded the paper, she stopped short. There on the front page was the story—and the headline:

"MURDER AT SOMERSBY TAVERN: LOCAL WOMAN QUESTIONED."

Margaret's throat went tight and she thought she would vomit. With an unsteady motion that suggested she might faint, she sat down in the nearest chair and with morbid curiosity read the entire story. The reporter described the scene and the fact that someone who had seen the "local woman" at the scene identified her to police.

"*Unnamed sources said today a letter found at the scene of the crime indicates that the victim and the local woman were having an affair. Police theorize that they argued after a confrontation concerning his alleged homosexual relationship with a Washington, DC man and the victim either shot himself or was murdered. Police would not confirm or deny the details of their investigation and the name of the victim was not released pending notification of his family.*"

"Thank God they didn't identify me, either," Margaret said aloud through tears, as her heart beat heavily in her chest.

Everyone was going to know about this, she sobbed, head dropping to the table in exasperation. Somebody saw her there...somebody who knew her. And somebody at the newspaper obviously knew who she was. Why didn't they release her name? And how long before they did? As she pondered these thoughts fearfully, the telephone was ringing. She stared at it for a moment, then reached up and removed the receiver from where it hung on the wall.

Jerry was calling from downtown. Their attorney, Jack Webster, had contacted him and Jerry had flown back immediately and was headed straight to his office. "Jack told me what happened. It must have been hell," Jerry said strangely, without emotion.

"I'm sorry, Jerry," Margaret wept silently, her voice nearly inaudible.

There was a terrible silence on the other end of the phone. Margaret clutched it tightly to her ear, hoping Jerry hadn't just simply hung up on her. Finally he spoke, his voice cold and harsh. "This guy was gay?"

Margaret bit her lip, still unable to believe it. "Yes," she answered, realizing that the very thing that had devastated her was the only thing that might save her marriage.

"And you knew it? Did Wes Crenshaw know? Was Ron always gay?" It was strange to remember suddenly that Jerry had known Wes and Dorothy Crenshaw and it was humiliating to be discussing Ron with Jerry.

"I don't know," she said curtly. "I don't know anything about their private family business."

"What the devil were you doing in his hotel room?" Jerry exploded in a tirade. "If you wanted to see the guy, you could have had dinner with him at a restaurant or brought him to the house. Did you have to go in his room? And there was Mildred Reeves, biggest mouth in the state of Indiana, in the lobby of that damned tavern just in time to see you rush out of there like you'd been shot—" Jerry stopped short at the realization of the irony of what he'd just said. "How in the name of Jesus Christ did you get involved in all this? This isn't the end of it, Margaret. I hope you realize that. There's going to be a full investigation…there will be reports in the paper—using our names. *My* name: Margaret. There will be a hearing and God knows what else. What have you done to my life?" Jerry was shouting so loudly Margaret held the receiver away from her ear.

She deserved everything he was saying and more. She'd brought shame and humiliation upon her family because of her selfish desire to recapture something that could never have been anyway. She wanted to die.

"I've worked twenty-two years to make a name for myself," Jerry went on no less loudly, "to build a reputation. To become somebody. And in one fell swoop my wife—the person who is supposed to stand by me through thick and thin, the person who should be my best supporter; someone I can be proud of and show off—my so-called 'wonderful' wife goes and gets involved with a fag and a murder investigation. My reputation is shot to hell. Do you realize that? Shot to hell!"

There was a deafening silence, as Margaret slid down the wall and onto the kitchen floor, still clutching the phone.

"See you at home," Jerry hissed, and slammed the receiver down.

Chapter 20

Margaret stumbled out the kitchen door and stood at the porch railing. The night was warm, the stars bright and distinct. Someone on another street was barbecuing and the aroma of steaks and hot dogs wafted on a gentle breeze through the trees. She heard laughter and it sounded foreign to her soul. What was happiness? Had she ever known it? She sat heavily in one of the lounge chairs and took purposeful sips from the iced tea glass she'd filled to the top with scotch, and sank slowly into a deeply relaxed state. It was in this fog of oblivion that she began walking mentally through the events of the past twenty-four hours, from the moment Ron escorted her into his room at Somersby Tavern through her painful realization that Brent might be Ron's child to the just-ended conversation with Jerry.

She closed her eyes and thought about the ramifications of Ron being Brent's biological father. No, she thought shaking her head defiantly. Brent is Jerry's child. They look alike, they walk alike. Her heart would not accept anything else. But what kind of life had she been leading—so much of it a lie.

And Ron was dead; she tried to recapture the inviting comfort she had known in Ron's arms where she had felt secure. Setting her glass down, she involuntarily reached both arms around herself in an effort to recapture the warmth of his embrace. Then, just as she began to feel peace in her soul, the question Jerry spat at her rang loudly in her mind: *"The guy was gay?"*

She shook her head to escape from the realities that plagued her. Gay men do not take female lovers. Ron couldn't have been gay. Ginny had suggested that Ron was bisexual. To Margaret, that didn't make acceptance easier. There had to be some other explanation. Margaret could not understand, yet she could not stop loving him; at least not the man she knew, the man she remembered all those years...that was the man she loved and cherished secretly in her heart.

Several times Margaret fell asleep in her chair, the half-empty glass nearly slipping from her hand, but she would abruptly awaken and take another long swallow. It felt good to be drunk. The pain was dulled.

She heard the phone ringing. Like some distant call of a baby crying, it persisted in her brain. One ring. Two. She tried to stand up, but her legs were weak. Four, five rings. She finally stopped fighting her unwilling body and waited for the answering machine to pick up the line, listening, eyes half closed. They flew open when she recognized the voice:

"Mom," she heard Brent saying. "Jason drove Susan down here last night and they are going to be staying with me in Charlottesville for a few days. It's too—you know—too hard for them there right now. Everybody's okay and I've got plenty of room since both my roommates are gone for the summer. See you."

Margaret stared toward the house as she listened to her oldest boy talking. His usually carefree voice sounded so mature and capable. Mother and Father had shirked their duty; had let the children down; had failed. He, the oldest, was going to take charge. There was no question in his voice; no uncertainty. Margaret's bleary eyes glistened and her heart ached. How much did the children know, she wondered and again was cloaked in shame.

The pain quickly returned, sharp as if a knife had been pushed between her ribs. She had hurt her children. Jerry was no doubt gone from her life...Ron was dead. And God, if He even existed, didn't care anymore.

With a great sense of purpose she went back inside, stripped off her nightgown and pulled on a pair of summer jeans, a long-sleeved

Tee shirt and tennis shoes. Downing the last drop of scotch from her large tumbler, she headed out of the house.

Margaret had no plan, she just wanted to get away from the house, as if doing so would take her away from the desolation that had beset her. She did not want to be seen by the neighbors, so she headed for the back of the house toward the woods. Wild roses pulled at her jeans and low tree branches whipped her face as she walked unsteadily along, oblivious to anything but the ache in her heart. She wove in and out of obstacles, stepping through thick underbrush.

It was not a large wooded area, but large enough to wander in for a long time without emerging. She remembered Brent getting lost in here one time for most of a day when he was about 12 years old. He had been resourceful and found his way out by reading the signs taught him as a young Boy Scout... Just as he was being resourceful now and providing a way out for the two younger children who were seemingly lost in the mess she had created. The only thing she had ever cared about being was a good mother. She's spent twenty years being that mother, thinking only of her children, gladly giving up a life of her own and even, perhaps, a closer relationship with her husband for those children. And in one weak moment, she'd undone all the good she might ever have accomplished.

The scotch dulled her mind, but it would not dull the pain. The night air, heady with the fragrance of wisteria, was clearing her thoughts. She stopped to get her bearings. Looking around, she knew she could head left and circle back around to the house, or right and end up at the river. The river called to her.

Though she wanted to forget everything, thoughts of Ron filled her mind. His warmth, his caring, these were things that drew her to him in the first place and that still made her long for him. Despite anything, the person she knew she loved. Whatever road Ron had taken, he had carried a part of her with him; and a part of him remained with her now. She was to blame, she was sure, for his retreat to a life she couldn't understand; perhaps she was also to blame for his death.

Guilt overwhelmed her; guilt for what she had done to Ron, for what her children would have to put up with, with the upcoming, very public trial that would drag everyone through the mud. She felt guilt for what she had done to Jerry and what he would have to face, for in spite of everything, her feelings for Jerry had not changed. He was her husband, the father of her children. She would not have left him, not even for a life with Ron. She loved Jerry; not perhaps in the way she had loved Ron, but despite everything, she would never have wanted to hurt Jerry. Not like this.

Margaret's thoughts turned for a moment to her friend Ginny Ashwell. Ginny had been such a strong supporter throughout their years of friendship. Margaret and Ginny had shared so much; had grown up as mothers together, learning to raise their children, and to be advocates for them in the school system. Ginny was like a sister to her; closer even than Cathy who because of the years and distance that separated them never seemed to share quite as easily. Yes, Margaret thought, even Ginny would be hurt by the trial. She imagined Ginny might even be called to testify and Ginny knew so many of Margaret's secrets…would she be forced to tell them?

Suddenly Margaret saw herself on the witness stand:

"Mrs. Ammons, you were with the deceased in his hotel room on the night of the murder?"

"Yes,"

"For what purpose were you in Mr. Crenshaw's hotel room?"

No response.

"Is it true, Mrs. Ammons, that you were having an affair with Mr. Crenshaw? And isn't it also true that Mr. Crenshaw had a male lover? And didn't that make you so angry that you pulled the trigger of his own gun and then tried to make it look like a suicide?"

Margaret saw the faces of her family and friends in the courtroom—faces harboring looks of dismay, embarrassment, sympathy for the pathetic woman she'd become. It was more than she could bear.

She hadn't pulled the trigger, but she may as well have killed him. She left him devoid of hope and it was too much for him. They would discover, soon, that it was suicide. Why it was taking so long for that, she didn't know. But it didn't matter. Even if they convicted her of the killing, what difference did it make now? In spite of the fact that she hadn't pulled the trigger, she knew she was responsible for Ron's death—a death that took more than twenty years to accomplish. A death that almost successfully ended that unfinished chapter.

She began running to escape her thoughts and the voices she heard screaming in her head—Ron, J.D., Jerry, the police. She heard Brent's unemotional voice telling her he was taking care of his brother and sister, the disapproval emanating from him breaking her heart. She rushed on through the brush trying to escape the thoughts that tumbled through her mind. With dry throat and heart pounding, Margaret stumbled forward into a clearing and found herself beside the river. Going to the edge of the bank, she watched transfixed as the water bubbled and boiled over rocks, carrying sticks and other debris along its way. She grasped a tree that was growing over the river and leaned down to put her hand into the current. The water was cold and unfriendly. She walked slowly on, low on the bank close to the water. She stopped a time or two, sometimes at places where the water seemed calmer, where she would stare into it and, in the moonlight, see the reflection of a broken spirit.

As she studied her face in the dark water, she had an overwhelming desire to reach out and grasp the reflection, that shell of what had once been Margaret Wood Ammons. Yes, Ron's death had almost finished the chapter, but Margaret knew as long as she was alive, the story would not truly be over. It would drag on and on, with more and more hurt throughout the coming years as her family moved farther and farther apart. Maybe she wouldn't go to jail, but she would be incarcerated within the tomb she'd created for herself. She'd be alone. No husband; no children. Probably no friends either.

And what kind of life would her children experience now? Ridicule? Would their friends be hostile? Would they find it wickedly humorous? Would Margaret's actions cause them to be ostracized in their own community?

The water didn't look unfriendly now; it seemed tempting; inviting. She wondered how long she would struggle if she jumped

EVEN NOW

in...would she just relax and let herself sink slowly into the depths, or would her natural instincts cause her to thrash about until, exhausted, the river dragged her down?

Tears tumbled down her face for the life that was ended—not Ron's, but her own. She shut her eyes and gave one last try at trying to imagine life ever being normal again. With stinging conscience, she knew it never would.

The thought of just floating along, weightless in the water coaxed her closer to the edge. It was peaceful to drown, she had always heard. Though how anyone knew, she didn't understand.

But peaceful or not, it was time for her to end the chapter. It was time to give her family something that would overshadow the affair and murder and cause people to show them sympathy for their lost mother and wife. She stepped carefully down the bank and into the dark rippling water. Her body resisted the cold but could not overrule the decision her mind had made. Soon she was floating, just as she had imagined; almost feeling her body was not her own. Gradually she got used to the coldness of the water and relaxed, allowing herself to be carried by the current. Oddly, she did not feel frightened. She felt she was doing something positive; something to redeem a horrible situation. It was a great irony to be able to hear the bells of Overstone Abbey calling the monks to mass as she floated past. So peaceful...

Gradually the thought of sinking beneath the water became a pleasant and acceptable one, though she knew she wasn't yet tired enough and she didn't want to struggle at the last minute. She would just continue on her journey until, too tired to resist, she sank into the depths of the river.

Margaret's body began to stiffen in the cold water and it became harder to mover her arms and legs which kept her afloat. It hadn't been a very warm spring, and even if it had, it usually took the river a long time to warm up to swimming temperature. That, and the large amount of alcohol she had consumed, began causing her confusion. At one point, she thought she was in bed, ready to sleep. She coughed as her mouth filled with water when she first slipped under, but it wasn't time yet. She reminded herself that she was not going to fight death. She was on a mission.

She was tired now. She wondered how long she had been in the river, but it didn't matter. She felt calm, relaxed. And somehow without pain. Nothing really mattered. Not Ron's death, not their affair. Nothing, she thought sleepily. In the end, nothing in this life matters. Her body didn't feel cold anymore. She was quite comfortable. It seemed a perfectly natural thing to be floating like this. So much more comfortable than the reality of life. The pain—the awful pain; the struggle, just to be good, to be right. Life was too hard. Death so much more simple. So easy…just drift away.

Slowly and without struggle she slipped beneath the surface.

Chapter 21

Jerry walked in the front door of his house and let it slam shut behind him to announce his arrival and his state of mind. He put his overcoat and briefcase in the hall closet, set the newspaper down beside his easy chair, and went to the kitchen to make a cup of instant coffee, turning on lights as he went. He wasn't surprised to see the house in total darkness; Margaret often went to bed early. He was surprised, however, to find an iced tea glass that smelled strongly of scotch on the kitchen table. In spite of everything going on, it didn't seem like Margaret's way of handling things. He made one last call to the office to check his messages then noticed the light flickering on the answering machine. He listened to the sound of his older son telling his mother that Jason and Susan were with him. Jerry frowned and hastily dialed Brent's number. Before anyone could answer, though, he hung up. It was just as well they weren't here right now, he thought. And he didn't want to get dragged into a conversation about the situation. There were too many questions; even his attorney, Jack Webster, didn't know what to make of it. Had the man committed suicide or had he been murdered? Seemed to Jerry it ought to be cut and dried; easy to determine suicide, wasn't it? Well, no matter. Margaret didn't kill anyone. Margaret didn't have that kind of passion.

He would have to find a way to get past this professionally though. Something like this could cause him real problems. He stirred cream into his coffee, tucked the paper under his arm and headed for his easy chair. Right now his biggest problem, though, was what to do with the children, he thought as he made himself comfortable. They couldn't stay with Brent very long. He had summer courses and his job, and Jerry didn't like the lack of supervision and the temptations of a college town looming before Susan and Jason. But for now he'd leave things as they were. He'd spent several hours talking to Jack Webster to get a feel for how this kind of thing played out. They'd discussed divorce, but Jack said it would be prudent to wait until after the trial. It was unreal, being involved in something like this. Jack hadn't been nearly as upbeat as Jerry thought he should have been, given that Margaret was almost certainly just an innocent bystander in the whole thing. Margaret, who never hurt anybody, was probably there to try in her misguided way to help her old friend Ron Crenshaw. There was no way she was involved physically. The reports were simply wrong.

Still, he had his career to think of, and the children. He'd long ago learned that truth didn't matter; it was perception that was everything, and the perception of his wife had changed. He would have to consider separation and divorce. Jason would be off to college soon, and if Susan knew the entire story, she'd probably not want to stay with her mother. Jerry realized none of them probably knew the entire story. He hoped they never did.

He opened the paper and his eyes came immediately to rest on the story titled "Murder at Somersby Tavern." He read it quickly then lowered the paper, eyes smarting. Blinking hard, he drained the last of his coffee and headed for the door. He didn't know where he was going, but he had to leave the house. He couldn't stay there with Margaret; not tonight.

Jerry went outside to his car, which he'd parked just behind Margaret's, started it and backed out the circular drive. Without any plan, he headed down the road, out of their sub development, down past the high school and along the river. Feelings of inadequacy crept over him, as did grief, for what he wasn't sure. Perhaps it was for what he'd lost, but his mind kept taking him back to his childhood when his father's stern countenance was ever before him. Images of himself in the dark basement, or closet, or wherever his father determined would "strengthen" him, came tumbling through his mind, one after the other.

As a child, he'd done well at school under the harsh discipline of his father and the constant criticism of his mother. He'd gotten away from them as quickly as possible, and made it to the top in business. He'd even married his high school sweetheart—won her back... He stopped for a moment, wondering about that. "How'd I win her back?" He questioned, searching his memory in an area he'd seldom given any thought to.

He remembered dates with Margaret that year; few and far between. He'd dated other girls too, but Margaret had been an enigma and there was something mysterious about her that had drawn him to her. She was a challenge and Jerry always was up for a challenge.

He remembered the night he proposed to her and she accepted. His thoughts drifted back to their walk around the Tidal Basin in Washington, DC and their lovemaking hidden under the branches of a cherry tree. After that, she seemed to change overnight, from a woman who seemed always distracted to one totally focused on him. It was heady stuff for the young Jerry Ammons.

Then, after they were married, Margaret's total commitment to him transferred to the children. As each baby came, she had less time for him. A motherly Margaret did not appeal to him, so Jerry distanced himself and was drawn to other women. At first it was minor flirtations, but later it became a regular routine to find a woman who was challenging and finally break through the ice. Like Abigail. He had been particularly drawn to Abigail who became even more interesting once she was engaged to Charles. Abigail was a whiz at her job, businesslike and capable. Jerry admired that and went after it.

Now, in the cold hard reality facing him, Jerry felt a twinge of guilt. Was he somehow responsible for this mess they were in? Or, was it both of them? In spite of Margaret's outward virtue, there were, Jerry knew, skeletons in her closet too. After all, she had been pregnant when they married. He'd gone ahead and married her in spite of that fact. He'd done his job; his duty. He remembered his first thought was to run. He didn't have a good job and his well-planned future didn't include a baby right away. But he'd done what was necessary.

He'd provided a good home for his family. Everything they could possibly need or want he had given. How could Margaret betray him like this?

Had she murdered the guy? Was Margaret capable of that? No, he thought again. Not possible. But even if she hadn't, but was found guilty of the crime, she would be locked away. Imagine the embarrassment to the kids—and himself. He wondered about when to divorce her. Should he start the proceedings before the trial, or try to maintain some sort of public pretense until everything was over, then quietly divorce her and leave town. Start over.

He could go wherever he wanted; no doubt he'd lose this job, but he'd find another. Maybe he'd like to start out in California. Or even back to DC. Maybe moving to California would be more exciting to the kids.

Jerry felt remorse for the fact that his children did not know him well. A feeling of failure crept over him. Abruptly he turned away from River Road, which followed the winding river through the woods behind their development, and he headed to the center of Indianapolis where Abigail lived. Just before he got to her house, he stopped at the corner store and called her from a telephone booth.

Abigail was friendly, but distant. "What do you need, Jerry?"

"I need a place to stay tonight. Is your couch vacant?" Jerry tried to sound jocular, but his voice was tense. He had slept on Abigail's couch more than once when they had worked late and he had taken her home, hoping for more than a cup of coffee or a nightcap.

"Jerry, Charles is here..."

Jerry cleared his throat and tried to sound casual. "Well, is he on your couch?" Jerry felt the unfamiliar sense of being rejected. He knew immediately that he sounded ridiculous. "Never mind, Abi..."

"No, come on over," Abigail relented. "Charles knows he doesn't have anything to be jealous of."

That hurt. It was one thing that Jerry and Abigail both knew there was nothing between them, but Jerry liked to make it look like there was. It made him feel good about himself to have illusions that Abigail found him irresistible. Tonight there was just too much reality.

"Nah, " Jerry said, pursing his lips and trying to sound strong. "I just thought you'd like a little company." He hung the receiver up and slipped back into the seat of his car, leaning his head on his steering wheel. Broken and alone, for the first time in a long time, he started wishing he could just go home and be with his wife.

He started the car and drove around Indianapolis and the outskirts of the city all night long. As the sun was rising he knew he couldn't go on any longer, so he pulled off the road by the woods near his house close to the river where locals pulled small fishing boats in and out of the water. There he fell asleep.

The noontime sun made the car unbearably hot. Jerry awoke with a start, glad he'd left his windows down or he might have suffocated. He thought cynically how Margaret would then have been left to deal with another death. Oddly, the thought wrenched his heart.

Straightening out his clothing, he ran a comb through his hair, put the car in gear and headed toward the nearest place with food. He thought a good meal would solve the emptiness that engulfed him. He drove on, turning down a winding country road and thought how beautiful and fresh everything was, how neatly kept the lawns and gardens of the unfamiliar community he was entering. It wasn't until he turned a corner and looked up the hill that he realized he had come upon Overstone Abbey. "Just what I need," he mumbled sarcastically. "How the hell do I turn around in this place?"

The road leading up to the Abbey was too narrow to turn around until he had pulled up beside the imposing sandstone building. At that point, the driveway circled around a large courtyard and headed back out. Hearing music emanating from inside, Jerry stopped the car and listened. From within the Abbey came the inspiring sound of men chanting the liturgy.

A desperate feeling of need crept over Jerry. He parked the car and walked toward the chapel where the monks clothed in brown robes were totally immersed in worship. It was disturbing to him. Scenes from his childhood began to cross his mind. He saw the tiny church his mother had taken him to that confirmed the angry God she taught him was always waiting to punish the evildoers. He saw his father, distant and demanding, the same as the God his mother portrayed. He heard his mother's constant condemnations, felt the crack of his father's wide belt as he "taught" Jerry to be strong. Other scenes flashed through his mind. The day he and Margaret got married, how loving she had been; the day Brent was born and the incredible joy he had felt to have a son. It was difficult to keep his emotions in check. He swallowed hard.

He was aware that the service had ended and that the monks had filed out, but he was rooted to the spot. He was right to be angry with Margaret. He had been betrayed, he reasoned. How could he ever get over that churning mass that his stomach became every time he thought of what Margaret had done?

But as he studied the scene out the window, low-cut, verdant lawns edged by colorful flower borders, Jerry felt something else— a conviction in his soul that he had caused this same kind of hurt in his wife.

"Hello, Brother," a short smiling fellow dressed in a long brown hooded robe said as he touched Jerry's arm. "Can I be of help to you?"

Jerry took a deep breath as he climbed out of himself back into the world. Reality came crashing down on him…he had not been there when Margaret needed him. He'd failed her in so many ways. And while he knew forgiveness would be hard, and perhaps he would never forget, he needed to put his family back together. Sitting there in the Abbey, he felt he at least needed to try.

"Can I do something for you?" the monk repeated.

"Yes," Jerry said, letting tears go for the first time since he was eight and his father had told him angrily that men don't cry. "Yes" he repeated with conviction. "You can pray for me."

Chapter 22

In the bright lights of the hospital room, Margaret opened her eyes and stared straight ahead. There she saw movement, but her foggy brain would not make sense of what she saw, neither would her ears tune into the sounds buzzing around her. With great effort, she turned her eyes toward the window and saw that it was light outside. She wanted to turn her head also, but her neck would not obey the command. Her eyes refused to stay open and she gave up the effort.

Her body felt like lead; her arms would not move. It was as though she were a thought process encased in heavy clay. "I failed," she thought wearily. "I failed even at this." Well, if she couldn't die, she could sleep and perhaps never emerge from that sleep. She closed her eyes and drifted off.

It was sometime later that she roused again, aware once again of movement and voices around her bed, but unwilling to leave her self-made cocoon. She kept her eyes shut against the world she no longer wished to be part of. And then a familiar voice broke through her bitterness.

"Mom?" It was Susan's voice that emerged from the din of other voices and sounds around her. Though Margaret longed to reach out and hold her youngest child, she couldn't. Her body wouldn't let her and her mind told her she had caused so much heartache that she didn't have that right. Instead she remained hidden under the cloak of apparent sleep.

She was supposed to be dead…to have drowned, to have peacefully slipped out of this terrible inner hurt that bore into her body reminding her of how she had damaged everyone she loved. What happened? Why was she still here to suffer the sight and sounds of her disillusioned children; the hatred of her husband; the sneers of the townspeople…the death of Ron. Everyone knew by now, she was sure, about Ron, about their affair. Did they still think she had killed him? Did she survive drowning only to face a judge and jury who would now surely think she was guilty and sentence her to die anyway?

"Mom?" Susan's plaintive voice tore at her heart. She could feel her daughter tentatively touch her hand. "Mom?"

Someone else entered the room. "How's she doing, Susan?" It was Ginny Ashwell; dear Ginny, taking charge in her firm but reassuring way. Margaret felt if she could face anyone, it would be Ginny. But not now, not with Susan present. There was too much shame.

"She's not responding to me," Susan said, voice cracking. "Or to Jason or Brent."

"She will," Ginny assured her.

"But why won't she?"

"It isn't that she won't, honey. She can't," Ginny stated in her knowledgeable way. Ginny had for years been part of the local town rescue squad and was more proficient than most of them still. "Remember, she's had a bad accident and the trauma has left her in a sort of coma. But the doctor's say she'll be all right. Don't worry, I promise she'll be fine. Where are Jason and Brent?"

"Downstairs at the snack bar. They were up here all morning and they were starving."

Margaret was startled to know that her sons had been with her and she hadn't even been aware of it. She jerked slightly, which caught Ginny's attention. Instead of bringing it to Susan's attention, though, she ushered her toward the door. "Let's go find the guys," Ginny suggested. "You need a break." Ginny glanced over her shoulder at Margaret as she continued to urge Susan to the hallway. Margaret wanted to speak but her mouth would not work and even her eyes would not cooperate now. She heard the door close behind Ginny and Susan and she struggled to open her eyes, but in vain. She could think more clearly now; her brain didn't seem as foggy. She tried to put things in perspective; tried to remember just exactly what had been happening.

Ron...Ron was dead...somehow. She, Margaret, was accused of murder...or perhaps they'd learned it was suicide. Jerry—Jerry was angrier than she'd ever heard him. By now, he may have lost his job. Certainly his relationship with J.D. Harkins was completely broken, because of her. All their business ventures together... Jerry would never want her around again, and would most probably want her out of the lives of the children, too. He'd be right; she didn't deserve to be part of their lives anymore. She had nothing left. Nothing to live for. Why in God's name hadn't she just drowned!

She thought of her mother and the kind of reaction she would have—and Cathy. Did they know, too? It was too much; she felt dirty and shamed. Exhausted, she once again she slipped into a deep slumber.

Her dreams were turbulent. At one point she saw Ginny, clothed fully in black, attending a funeral. Margaret realized it was her funeral and for some reason she resisted being dead. *It's what I want,* she thought as she roused. *Why should I care if I live or die now?* Sometime later she awoke. With great effort, she willed her eyes to open and succeeded. There, sitting beside her bed, was her mother. Ann Wood was glancing through a magazine and did not see her daughter open her eyes.

Margaret mouthed the word "Mom," but no sound came forth. However, the movement got Ann's attention. She rushed to her daughter.

"Peg," she cried. "Peg!" She leaned down and kissed her daughter's forehead. "It's Mom, Peg. Can you see me?"

Soon the room was filled with the children, Ginny, Ann's boyfriend Bill, and Cathy. All were staring at her as if expecting her to give a speech. It was frightening to have everyone she loved standing so close, obviously aware of her terrible deed. Though Margaret wanted to speak, she just could not. She could not even lift her hand to acknowledge them. A tear slipped down from the corner of her eye and onto the pillowcase.

A nurse bustled in and checked her blood pressure, temperature and pulse, then ushered everyone out of the room. "Too many people in here at one time. It's late. Let her sleep," Margaret heard the strong-willed woman say. "Come back tomorrow."

When the nurse herself stepped outside the door, she was met by Jerry, who identified himself. "May I see her?"

The nurse was clearly annoyed to have yet another intrusion. "For a minute. She's very tired and it's been an emotional day for her."

"The doctor told me she's in a coma."

"Something like that. Though she's opening her eyes and I think is aware of who's around her, at least sometimes. Go on in, but be sensitive to the fact that she might not respond. And she needs to rest."

Jerry cautiously opened the door and gazed at his sleeping wife from a distance. "Think of it as post-traumatic stress syndrome" the doctor had told him. Perhaps a self-induced coma, he had said. Definitely hypothermia: and perhaps pneumonia. Jerry stood awkwardly at the door, then slowly moved into the room and over to his motionless wife. "Hi, Margaret," he whispered. Not knowing whether or not she could hear him, he bend down and took her hand. "I'm sorry, Margaret," he said, voice cracking. "So sorry." He caressed her hand and then held it firmly in both of his. Then he sat in the chair beside the bed, absently caressing her wedding ring. "It's going to be all right," he assured her. His eyes were filling with tears, tears that had become far too familiar over the past hours. He pulled out his handkerchief and wiped them away.

For the first time in a long time, he studied his wife's face. Smooth skin, a slight upward turn at the corners of her bow-shaped lips, long dark lashes and heavy eyebrows. Her dark curly hair tumbled across her pillow. He was struck by how beautiful she was, even after all that had happened, and struck even more by the fact that he had barely bothered to look at her this closely in years. He had to leave; his emotions were raw from the conflict that raged within him over what she'd done and the good possibility he'd been the cause of it. He stood and brushed her forehead with his lips, then departed.

In spite of her desire to stay hidden deep within herself, by the next day Margaret was sitting propped up on her bed pillows. Ginny had stayed by her side all day, coaxing her back as if she fully understood the inner struggle Margaret was having. Ginny was a strong woman, with strength gained from years of struggle after a divorce left her to raise her children alone. She'd had to fight for everything she'd gotten over the years until she finally found success in her children's shop. She started when the children were small with a babysitting business she called "Ginny's Nursery." As her children grew and went off to school each day, she began "Ginny's Designs," clothing she made to order at home, squeezing the work in between raising the children, taking part in their school activities, being part of the PTO and taking care of the house. Never one to feel sorry for herself, Ginny worked hard "to prove herself," she often said. Her work was so good that in time she was able to open her own shop in town and that was what Margaret had recently become a part of. Many people wondered why Ginny always used her name no matter what her business was. "To affirm myself," was her honest answer. For in spite of how uplifting she could be to others, Ginny had a hard time feeling good about herself.

Now Margaret felt so much love for this friend who cared for her; who had always been there for her when there were problems and especially now, during this time, being a voice of reason, helping her children get through it. She reached out and squeezed Ginny's hand while the nurse took her vitals. "You know, Ginny. I dreamed you were at my funeral...and you looked terrible in black."

Ginny looked serious. "Then don't ever give me cause to wear it," she said firmly.

Margaret learned from Ginny that a man walking his dog late the night she stepped into the river saw her floating in the water and called the police, who had arrived just in time to see her go under. It was surprising to Margaret that she could be so physically affected by that one incident, and she expressed that to Ginny.

"It wasn't just one incident, Margaret," Ginny said earnestly. "You've been running on high since Dorothy Crenshaw's funeral. You had to come down sometime...It's just too bad you crashed and burned alone! Not to mention the fact that your body temperature had dropped severely from your little swim."

"Blood pressure is fine," the nurse smiled as she unwrapped the cuff from around Margaret's arm, removed the thermometer and wrote the information on her chart. "Someone will be back soon to get you up," she said, closing the door.

"So, how're you feeling today," Ginny asked when the nurse had left. "I mean really feeling?"

Margaret shrugged. "Like a fool."

Ginny rolled her eyes. "Honey, you've had one thing after another come down on you over the past few months. No one thinks you're a fool."

"I did a foolish thing."

Ginny gave a wink. "And which one thing are you calling foolish?"

"OK," Margaret laughed. "I did MANY foolish things. The kids, Ginny. I'm so worried about them. How they'll respond. What they'll think of me."

"You know what? The first thing is to stop thinking of them as 'kids,'" Ginny said, getting up and pouring juice in the plastic cup on Margaret's tray. "They're nearly grown. Even Susan is old enough to understand that parents are people too, who have emotions, pain and, most important, who make mistakes. Your children love you. There's no condemnation there."

Margaret smiled at her friend. "You always say the right thing." But in her heart, Margaret could not believe her.

"Has Jerry been here?"

Margaret shook her head. "But I dreamed he came in last night," Margaret said, not realizing he had in fact been there. "The way he acted in my dream reminded me of the old Jerry. Gentle. Emotional." Margaret smiled wistfully.

"Well, honey, I've got to run. Do you need anything before I go?"

Margaret thought for a moment. "You know what I'd really like? To get up to go to the bathroom. They're going to get me into a chair soon," she said. "Maybe you could just walk me over to the bathroom…"

"Not on your life without permission," Ginny said.

Margaret held up the call button attached to a cord hidden under the covers of her bed. "I'll just press this handy-dandy little device and get the nurse and ask her if you and I can walk to the bathroom." She pressed the button and a nurse soon appeared in the doorway. "Can my friend take me to the bathroom?" she asked.

The nurse went into the room. "We'll both take you," she offered. And together the women helped her up. Margaret was weaker than she anticipated, but finally she was settled in the chair beside the window where she could watch life going on outside the hospital walls. Sitting there watching traffic going by and people rushing about helped her step outside herself a little more.

The children came in that afternoon with Jerry, Cathy and Ann Wood. Margaret had been napping when they arrived and felt overwhelmed to have them all with her at one time. It was a time of stilted conversation and awkward silences. Separately they might each have had questions and she might have had answers, but together that kind of intimacy was impossible. She was grateful, though, that Jerry was with them and had not come alone, for she was not ready to have the conversation with him that they ultimately needed to have. She was much relieved when they were gone, though the empty room only served as a reminder of the void inside her body. She was too spent to cry, though tears found their way down her cheeks and her chest burned.

It had been an exhausting day. Hospital visiting hours were over and the halls emptied of people hurrying away, talking in hushed voices. Margaret lay in the darkened room watching the news, then clicked off the television and settled down for the night. As she was dozing, trying to sink back into that peaceful sleep she longed for that seemed to elude her now, she was haunted by visions of Ron. "Is that how it's always going to be?" she wondered. "Ron, living in my heart and mind forever?" She thought it ironic now that she felt better physically yet she couldn't sleep as well as when she was first brought to the hospital. She considered ringing the nurse for a sleeping pill. Tossing her covers around to get more comfortable, she became aware that someone was in the room watching her. It was a woman, vaguely familiar, standing and staring. Margaret reared up and instinctively pulled the covers over herself protectively. "Alice!" She cried aloud with sudden recognition.

Alice, the woman with whom Margaret had had that silly conversation at the Crenshaw house after Dorothy's funeral; the woman who shared a house with Ron. The woman who loomed mysteriously in Ron's life, because he never talked about her, only occasionally mentioned her name. Hearing her name, Alice moved closer to the bed. She looked strange; tired, much older than she had when Margaret met her at Dorothy's funeral.

"Hello, Margaret," Alice said, her voice deep and her words slow.

"Hello!" Margaret stammered, sliding fully into a sitting position, still clutching the covers across her chest.

"I see you're recovering. That's good." Alice moved closer and to Margaret's great surprise reached out and hugged her tightly. For a long moment the woman held her in silence. Then, standing back, Alice spoke. "I had to do that. You see, Ron would have wanted me to...You really did love him, didn't you?"

Margaret lowered her eyes. It was not a matter she cared to discuss with anyone, let alone Alice. And she didn't know really what Alice's relationship with Ron had been.

"You shouldn't be ashamed of it," Alice went on, becoming agitated. She sat down in the steel and leather visitor's chair and pulled it closer to Margaret's bed. "I'm jealous of you, you know. All these years...if it hadn't been for you..." she stared intently at Margaret unwilling to finish her sentence.

Margaret felt very uncomfortable. Alice was a foreboding woman; she had been that way at the funeral. But now, in the dark in Margaret's hospital room under these circumstances, Margaret felt all too vulnerable.

"I loved him too," Alice said. "You probably knew that."

"I—no, I didn't," Margaret responded

"Not many people knew. But I really was part of the family. I went to every family function. I was like a daughter to Ron's parents."

Margaret nodded as if she understood.

Alice tilted the chair back, pulling the front legs off the floor and rocking back and forth, eyes hard on Margaret.

"Wes Crenshaw asked me to come to identify the body. He was too devastated to make the trip. I was like a daughter to Wes. Did you know that?" Alice had a strange, hollow expression.

Margaret shook her head, praying Alice would leave.

"And I know something you would be surprised to know…" she went on, a self-satisfied look coming over her face.

Margaret waited, wondering what kind of game Alice was playing, wondering if the woman was sane. She seemed unbalanced. The look in her eyes frightened Margaret. And though Alice was small in stature, she looked formidable.

Margaret remembered when she saw Alice for the first time, how she thought the woman was strange then. But that whole situation had been strange. Now Margaret knew her instincts had been right; though she'd never put it in words, she suspected Alice's friendship with Ron went deeper than simply house mates. Alice had been in love with Ron. Margaret wondered if he had ever reciprocated her love.

"Yes, I was like a daughter to Wes Crenshaw," Alice went on, talking more to the window beyond Margaret than to Margaret. "And I was the one he wanted to come here and make the identification. Wes Crenshaw asked me to come. I was to identify his son, and take…his son…home." Alice blinked several times and then her eyes moved from the window back to Margaret. "So I went down to the morgue; awful place. Just awful. I did it for Wes. He was like a father to me. I should have been his daughter-in-law. Well, anyway, I went. For Wes. I had to be strong, for Wes. And I went in and stood there and they brought the body out of the freezer…on that long gurney, covered in a white sheet…I was afraid. I wanted to run away. But I kept thinking I had to be brave, for Wes." Alice took a deep breath and her lips formed a big, eerie smile. "And when they pulled back the sheet and showed me the body, I laughed. Oh, I tried not to, but I laughed so hard I nearly fell over!'

Margaret drew back, terrified, as Alice's voice grew shrill.

Alice clamped her lips into a line and nodded with self-satisfaction. "Yes, dear, sweet Margaret. I tried to be cool and collected so they wouldn't know I already knew the truth, but I laughed. I laughed at the stupidity of the police. At the stupidity of Ron who never returned my love. At the stupidity of the whole situation. I couldn't hold it in any longer. I nearly fell over I laughed so hard. Stupid cops. What did they know? But I knew. It was a perfect crime!

"Someone heard a shot; they found a body in Ron's room, with Ron's luggage. With Ron's letter to you... They found your address book. All the signs that the victim was Ron Crenshaw." Alice put her face close to Margaret's, her acrid breath blanketing her face. "It was not Ron, Sweetie. But the cops didn't know that and I wasn't going to tell them. It was Joe! Joe Harkins who was dead!" Alice laughed again, loudly, and her voice rose again. "It was Joe! And they never knew. How I hated Joe. The too-good-for us all J.D. Harkins. He was a millstone around Ron's neck. I hated the man. And there he was in the morgue dead as a doornail. He got what he deserved." Alice laughed again the bitter, hateful laugh of revenge. "Do you understand what I'm telling you, you useless female?" she seethed at Margaret. "It wasn't Ron who died in that room."

Margaret couldn't believe what she was hearing. She couldn't speak. Alice seemed close to hysteria, yet her words rang true. It wasn't Ron who died. If Ron wasn't dead, where was he? Why had he disappeared? Then suddenly she knew—the full impact of what Alice had told her. The ramifications of all this. Ron must have killed Joe. New pain surged through Margaret searing through the dull ache and stabbing like a knife in her heart.

Alice strutted dramatically around the room. "All I could ever be to Ron was a friend. I learned that early on. Oh, we met long before Joe was on the scene. We worked in the same building. In fact, we even dated awhile. But after a few months, when Ron hadn't even kissed me goodnight, I knew something was wrong. It was clear he liked me; he always wanted me around. We even bought that house together. But there was something within him holding him away from me." She stopped by Margaret's bed and leaned close again. "Do you know what was haunting Ron...keeping him from loving me?" she shoved her finger into Margaret's chest. "You."

Breathing hard, Alice began pacing rapidly back and forth at the foot of the bed. "Not Joe. No, Joe was an escape. Something sure; comfortable. Joe was no threat to me. It was you. You were a specter always on the scene. He talked about you when I first met him. And as years went by, he talked about you even more. And since the funeral, you'd think there was no other subject. The man was possessed.—No, *I'm* the one who's possessed. He was obsessed. Obsessed with you. Can't imagine why. You don't look like anything special to me. Do you think you're special?" Alice leaned down close to Margaret's face and studied her from about a foot away.

Margaret could contain herself no longer. "Where is he? Do you know where Ron is? Do the police know?"

"All these years," Alice went on without hearing, lost in herself, "All these years I just kept hoping one day he'd love me even a little bit. A little bit would have been enough. But no. No, he had some crazy idea that one day you'd be free and you'd still want him. And sister, you fooled the hell out of me. I was sure you hadn't given him another thought." Alice sat heavily on the chair and hung her head. "You surely fooled me," her tone became low, menacing.

Fearfully, Margaret felt for the nurses' call button, her hand clutching wildly for the cord, but she couldn't find it and she dared not let Alice know she was seeking it. Her heart was pounding hard as though it would burst through her chest as her hand searched frantically. Finally she felt the cord and grabbed for it just as the button fell off the side of her bed. Surreptitiously pulling at it back up under the covers, she pressed the button hard.

"Can I have a drink of your water?" Alice asked, not waiting for an answer. She downed the entire bottle. "Ahh. That was good...

Aren't you even curious to know who killed Joe?" Alice asked, in a surprisingly calm tone.

Margaret licked her lips nervously. "Yes, of course," she whispered, glancing toward the door hoping to see someone responding to her call. They were always so very slow at night.

Alice reached into her purse and retrieved a small weapon, a gun so small it was nearly hidden in her hand. "I did." She flung her head back proudly and twirled the tiny pearl-handled gun on her index finger. "Does that surprise you?"

Margaret gasped and drew back. She pushed the button again and again.

"Yes, I did it. When I was at the morgue, I intended to claim it was Ron, but my emotions got the better of me. They suspected something was wrong. But I'm too smart for them. I told them it wasn't Ron, but I didn't say I knew who it was. I had to tell them it wasn't Ron...otherwise my laughter would have seemed too strange and I didn't want to appear strange. I'm good aren't I? Quick at making decisions." Alice waited for a response, but Margaret was desperately trying to appear calm while ringing the button for help.

"Yes, I'm good," Alice went on. "You see. Ron told me everything. He told me he was coming here to see you. So I came here too, and went to Somersby and took a room down the hall from Ron's. I intended to kill him. If I couldn't have him, no one was going to have him, least of all you. I was tired of the game. It was easy to get one of his guns—we often went target shooting together. I thought it would be great to kill him with his own gun." Her voice was calm, as if she were talking about plans for a dinner party. "So I waited until I heard the door slam—I thought that was you leaving. See, I knew you were in there. Imagine if you'd stayed the night. I'd have been right there and maybe got you too! But you already left. I found that out when I went to the door of his room and heard Joe yelling at him. The more Joe yelled, the madder I got. Who the hell did he think he was anyway? I had wanted Joe out of the way for so long, I changed my plan right then and there. You didn't really matter. I could tell you didn't have the guts to leave your family; you weren't that kind. You

EVEN NOW

would soon be just a memory again and I'd learned to live with that. But Joe...Joe was a problem.

"So I went back to my room and waited. I knew Ron would leave. He always avoided fights. I knew him so well..." Alice looked wistfully off into the distance for a moment, then turned again to Margaret. "And I was right—of course. Ron stormed out the room and down the stairs. Joe didn't go after him; he never did. He knew eventually Ron would come back. At least, he always had before. So I waited a few minutes then went and knocked on the door. Joe naturally thought I was Ron and he threw the door open," Alice laughed that eerie laugh again.

"You should have seen his face when he saw me!" This time she laughed loudly, then suddenly stopped and looked around quickly to see if anyone in the hall had heard her. Then she drew herself up to her full height and strutted around demonstrating her crime. "I walked right into his room...right up to him...and I pulled the gun out of my purse and put it to Joe's head and before he knew what was up, I shot him! Then when he fell, I pushed his dead fingers around the gun and left. I wore gloves, just like they do in the movies and I put my gloves in a paper bag, wadded it up and tossed it into the garbage outside the Tavern. I flew back to Washington, DC that night, went home and went to bed. And that's where I was when Wes telephoned me later the next day."

Margaret frantically pushed the call button and clutched the covers around her body, knowing there was nothing more she could do. Alice studied the tiny gun in the palm of her hand. "I was hoping they'd think it was suicide, but it was a wonderful twist that they thought for so long the victim was Ron. Even I hadn't counted on that. That was the reason I was able to get away with it so easily. They were on the wrong trail. They thought you did it." Alice ominously raised the gun toward Margaret and squinted one eye. "Now I just don't think I can leave you to the criminal justice system; I think I have to get rid of you myself." Alice continued to level the gun at Margaret, who could only stare back at her in horror.

Suddenly the room was filled with people, all acting in unison. A detective dressed as an orderly grabbed Alice as she pulled the trigger. The shot went wildly into the air. A nurse rushed protectively over to Margaret, and two policemen escorted the cursing Alice out the door. As the nurse was trying to calm Margaret, a tall gray-haired man walked in the room. It was Jack Webster.

"How did you know to come?" she asked Jack weakly when he came over to her and took her hand.

"The police have been watching that woman since she arrived to identify the body. When the nurse came to your room to answer your call she heard Alice laughing and knew something was wrong. She telephoned the police and the police got hold of me. She's one weird chick!" Jack said, squeezing Margaret's hand.

"I'm so confused," Margaret said. "Can you help me understand all this?"

"Later, when you're home," Jack said. "For now, just know that all charges against you have been dropped."

There was so much more Margaret needed to know. So many questions. But for now it was enough to know that Ron wasn't dead and she wasn't a murderer.

Chapter 23

With a great determined purpose, Jerry drove like a madman through the streets of his small town to get home—home, where he had been but a visitor for too long. The day was hot and humid; he hadn't slept in more than twenty-four hours as he'd walked the streets searching for a purpose to his life. His clothes were rumpled; they smelled of sweat. His hair was disheveled and his dark, handsome face sported several days of stubble.

He'd spent time thinking, trying to work through the events that led to the situation he now faced. Not simply what had happened with Margaret over the past months, but his own focus in life. Margaret had been in the hospital less than a week. During that time, he, Jason and Susan spent time together, "hanging out," as Jason would call it. He realized clearly that he didn't know these wonderful people with whom he'd lived all their lives. They were thoughtful, insightful, intelligent and creative. And they loved their mother unconditionally. Jerry realized that was what love was all about…no conditions. No expectations. Margaret had been the kind of wife who let him do and be and become. Now, he hoped, he could learn to be the kind of husband who could do that for her. His pride was wounded; she had loved someone else. But he had worked through that. He only hoped it wasn't too late.

Ann Wood had stayed at the house for a few days after Margaret got home from the hospital. She'd left only yesterday. And Brent had gone back to Charlottesville. But Jerry had not been home at all. He slept in the office, where he'd spent a great deal of time working on the legal ramifications of his association with the now deceased J.D. Harkins. Ann had known Jerry planned to leave for good. She had seen it in his eyes and she told him she understood. It was hard for a man to accept a wife's unfaithfulness, she had told him. Women were expected to forgive. Men were not. Now, as he thought of those words, he wished he had told her that was crap. That men and women hurt just the same over such things and that he wished he'd learned that years ago. Ann was an unusual mother-in-law. He would tell her that one day, but right now he had to get things straightened out with Margaret. He only hoped it wasn't too late.

He turned squealing wheels into the driveway of his home and bounded up onto the porch where Susan and Margaret were sitting on the swing. Susan frowned at her father, and Jason appeared at the door. He stepped outside protectively, ready to confront his father. Jerry recognized this in his son's stance and he was proud of him.

"Susan, Jason, I want to talk with your mother. Go inside." They glanced at their mother, then glared at their father without moving.

"Please, kids," he said looking from one to the other. "Leave us alone. This is important."

Margaret nodded to her daughter and the girl got up and left. Jason lingered, then gave his father a glance that indicated he was ready to do battle if necessary, and he reluctantly closed the door behind him.

"Hi," Jerry said when they were alone, suddenly at a loss for words. He sat on an aluminum lawn chair across from his wife. "You look like you feel much better."

"I do," Margaret smiled, avoiding his eyes.

"We need to talk," Jerry said earnestly. "Or rather, I need to talk."

"You want to move back in," Margaret stated flatly. She knew Jerry would probably decide that. He was too success-oriented in everything he did to admit defeat in his marriage. Margaret had suspected he'd ask to come back for that reason, but also because it was the financially prudent thing to do. She guessed that one day in the near future, he'd suggest to her that she be the one to leave. Then it wouldn't be his failure, it would be hers. She'd spent hours deciding what she'd do under those circumstances and she decided that for the children's sake, she'd just go quietly along, taking one step at a time. "There's room."

Jerry shook his head. "We can't just go back to our life as it was and pretend nothing's happened."

"I didn't expect to, Jerry. I just thought you'd want to be here...it's your house."

Jerry stood up. "It's our house. But that's not what I'm saying either."

Margaret looked up at him. "Jerry, I'm too tired to debate. If you want to move in, move in. It will be better for the children. Please don't play verbal games with me any more."

"I'm not playing games, Margaret. I'm just having a hard time being humble. What I'm saying is, I want to move in, but not just for convenience. I want to work on 'us.'"

Margaret was totally unprepared for that and was immediately filled with guilt and shame. "Why would you want to have anything to do with me?" she questioned, biting her lip to keep from weeping.

Jerry reached down and took her hands in his. He gently pulled her to her feet, then held her chin and looked her dead in the eye. Nervously, he began the speech he had so carefully rehearsed. "Because you and I are more than one incident or one moment in time. Because we have a history together. Because you've been a wonderful wife and I haven't been such a wonderful husband." Once he got started his words poured forth dramatically and built with emotion as he said each sentence. "We need to try again because we have children together. Our future, yours and mine, will continue to include each other because of those children, even if we're living apart, even if we're divorced. We'll have weddings and grandchildren to bear witness to our union. No matter how far apart we might move from each other, the illness of a child, the birth of a grandbaby, the death of one of our parents—all this would bring us back together. And I know that for me that would be painful...to see you over and over and not belong to you anymore.

"I almost lost you, twice for God's sake. I'm not talking about to that guy; I'm talking about to death. You nearly drowned and that deranged woman nearly shot you. I can fight a man; I can't fight death.

"I remember when I was a teenager and I felt so helpless under my dad's threats and my mother's thumb. I wanted to die. Believe it or not, things got so hopeless I considered drowning myself in that very same way…but in the Potomac River. I really understand what you've been through—some of it, anyway, and I'd like for you to help me understand the rest."

Jerry wiped tears that were cascading down Margaret's cheeks. She didn't speak a word, and he was glad; he needed to go on, nearly afraid he was already too late.

"We need to try again, because…" he gulped nervously. "Because I love you very much." Jerry was choking up; he had to stop talking.

Margaret couldn't believe what she was hearing. Speechless, she waited for whatever else was on his mind, but he held back, unable to say the other words he had practiced: that he'd had one night stands and a couple of affairs in their twenty years of marriage; that he hadn't been a faithful husband. He just couldn't say those things that had been gnawing at him most in the past few days. Maybe someday he could, but not right now.

Now he needed to convince Margaret that he had put his life in proper perspective. That he didn't want to lose her. That even if they lost everything, including their reputations in this town; they needed to be together. And he knew he had no fortitude to rebuild his life unless she was in it with him.

Margaret could only nod her head. Feelings for Jerry that had been buried deep underneath the years of debris began to push to the surface. Margaret's heart leaped at the possibility they might begin again.

Ron wasn't dead, but he was gone. His father seemed to know where he was, but had told her mother Ron had relocated and was rethinking his life. Wes Crenshaw had seemed relieved but unwilling to say more, Ann Wood told Margaret. She said Ron had specifically asked his father to keep any further information from Margaret. Whether or not that was true, whatever happened in that hotel room at Somersby Tavern that night had taken him far away. Perhaps Margaret's rejection of him played as large a part in his disappearance as the death of Joe and the realization of Alice's true nature. Margaret would always hold Ron's memory closely in her heart, but she knew even if Jerry and she had divorced she would never have been able to make a life with Ron. He was to become simply one of those romances that linger in the heart long after the two people have moved on.

Jerry stood watching Margaret's face, hoping for some sign that she would give him a chance to be the person he wanted to be. She smiled at him and he slipped his arms loosely around her waist. They stood together awkwardly as if it were their first date. She leaned shyly against his shoulder, still unable to forgive herself; unable to fully let go of the nightmare she had created. When she pulled away and looked him directly in his eyes, she saw his eyes that were moist...something she had never seen in him before. His countenance was different, no longer confident and haughty; the chip on his shoulder gone. She saw in him a man who had experienced the good and the bad in life, had sorted the wheat from the chaff and knew what he wanted. And amazingly, he wanted his family to be whole. How could she want anything less?

Love welled up for him. Not the passion she had felt for Ron that had been built up in her lonely imagination for more than twenty years, but a love that was deep and grounded in all the things that matter.

"Thank you, thank you," she whispered as she pressed her cheek against his. She was comforted with the feelings that come from being close to someone familiar. There were other feelings creeping in, feelings of anticipation at the opportunity they had to develop a deeper relationship out of the pain they had caused each other and themselves.

Not long ago she had thought Ron was her second chance at life; now she knew she had been wrong. She didn't need second chances. Jerry was her life.

With unaccustomed shyness, she slipped her arms around Jerry's neck and touched his cheek with her lips. The sun had set on the horizon, streaking the sky with long orange fingers. A gentle breeze rustled the tops of the tall old evergreens in their front yard. Overhead a pair of geese announced their move to another location, and an owl called out from somewhere in the distance.

To Margaret, it seemed the whole earth had been on hold, waiting for them to get their lives back in order.

Epilogue
2004

Margaret walked to the top of what was becoming a very familiar grassy hill in a cemetery near Washington, DC. Since her father died, she'd been here now five times for funerals. Eleven years before, she'd lost her own mother and Jerry, both in the same year; both to cancer. She had come now to attend Wesley Crenshaw's funeral alone. Her sister, Cathy, who had married and was living across the country, hadn't come.

Margaret was now nearly 62 years old. She stood by her car looking down at the scene unfolding at the gravesite, where Wesley Crenshaw would be laid to rest. More than two decades had passed since she'd stood on this ground for Dorothy Crenshaw's funeral. She hadn't approached any of the family at the church. She knew so few of them now and it hadn't seemed right to intrude. She thought of course Ron would be with them, but he was not. Perhaps by now he, too, was gone.

Now it was spring; a gentle breeze rustled through the newly green trees. Color was splashed all around; yellow forsythia and pink, red and purple azaleas all looked glamorous against the closely cropped carpet of green lawn. Slowly she strolled along the road, always looking to her left, never losing sight of the place where Dorothy and Wesley Crenshaw would be forever side by side. So many memories. She smiled wistfully. How wonderful had been the eleven years she and Jerry shared together after her near drowning. Every day they had been grateful for their second chance. At first there had been so much regret for lost time that they couldn't get on with life, but time sorted all that out. They'd even bought a place in the Blue Ridge Mountains where they spent summers with the kids. Margaret still gathered there with them and their families. It was a place filled with love and good memories. Occasionally she went there alone; she'd come to know many of the residents of the small town of Crescent Rock, Virginia, and they'd been there for her after Jerry died. Coming late into their lives, those people knew Jerry differently than their friends in Overstone. She allowed that image of him to remain there in Crescent Rock, never wanting to relive any of the pain of their turbulent first twenty years together. She had only shared with one young woman there, herself in turmoil over a man, hoping to help her avoid some of what Margaret had gone through. The relationship she and Jerry discovered after they renewed their marriage had been wonderful, not only for Margaret, but also for the children.

She always wondered about Ron, though. How mysteriously he had just disappeared. She had to admit that there had been moments when she'd been dismayed that he hadn't tried to contact her, if only to tell her what his new life had brought him. But in time she realized that it had been for the best that the separation had been total.

Margaret stood still again, allowing the fragrant spring breeze to ruffle her silver-tinged dark curls, which still adorned her age-softened face. Staring at the gravesite, she wondered if she could generate enough power to conjure up Ron from wherever he had gone after their final meeting at Somersby Tavern. She knew if Ron were anywhere in the area, or if it had been at all possible, he would have been at his father's funeral. There were hundreds of people there, but Ron would have been with the family...and he hadn't been.

It was painful to think that Ron, too, might be dead, for Ron had always been so vibrantly alive in her heart. And Margaret had loved him so intensely. Even now...even knowing about his life with Joe, after all this time, she felt love for him. It wasn't an addiction, it wasn't a so-called fatal attraction, it was simply a place in her heart dedicated solely to him. In those brief moments they had together,

Ron had given her something special. Oddly, it was that special something that had successfully sparked her marriage back to life.

She wished she could tell Ron that; she thought he would probably be pleased to know it.

From where she stood, the voice of the priest echoed upward as he spoke words of comfort to the few who had come to the burial place: "Man that is born of a woman, hath but a short time to live, and is full of misery. He cometh up, and is cut down, like a flower; he fleeth as it were a shadow, and never continueth in one stay. In the midst of life we are in death; of whom may we seek for succor, but of thee, O Lord, who for our sins is justly displeased? Thou knowest, Lord, the secrets of our hearts; shut not thy merciful ears to our prayer; but spare us...suffer us not to fall from thee..."

Thou knowest the secrets of our hearts, the priest had said. The words rang in Margaret's ears and today that knowledge brought comfort rather than guilt.

As the service closed, Margaret stopped to watch three monks crossing the graveyard. She had noticed them earlier at the funeral. It wasn't unusual that there would be brothers there, for the Crenshaws were long standing members of the Catholic community. There had been nuns there, too, along with several priests who had not participated in the service but who had known the Crenshaws throughout the years. Garbed in brown, large hoods covering their bowed heads, the three brothers walked in silence from the Crenshaw grave. Though the day was warm, a shiver ran up Margaret's spine. Her mind wandered as she began remembering details of that beautiful, snowy December in 1963 when she stepped into a wonderful fantasy world with Ron who went in one instant from the boy across the street to the man she would always love. Involuntarily, she hugged her arms against her body. Theirs had been a strange relationship, but one never to die in her heart. She sat on a nearby bench, remembering.

On a hill just behind her one of the monks lingered at a distance, watching her. The others wandered off, leaving him to his thoughts. Though they didn't know of his pain, each of them knew the other had a private past that had brought him into the monastery, and they allowed those secret parts to remain hidden. Now at his request and without question they left Ron Crenshaw, the man they'd come to know as Brother Timothy, to work out that which had been hidden.

He hadn't seen Margaret in all these years, but he'd never stopped thinking about her. It had been to this Abbey he ran when he left Joe alone in that room at Somersby Tavern, and it was within these walls that he'd finally found inner peace. But he'd never forgotten Margaret. Now he looked lovingly at the woman who had so captivated his life.

He'd made his father promise to keep his whereabouts a secret, not just from Margaret, but from everyone; it had been Ron's desire to rethink who he was and make something good and decent out of his life, for the sake of his mother; for the sake of his sanity. But through his father, he'd kept abreast of Margaret's life until Ann Wood died, then there had been no way to know what she was doing. For many years he told himself he would find her as soon as he felt ready for yet another reunion. But even after he'd heard Jerry had passed on, Ron hadn't been ready. Maybe he never would be.

As he stood silently, caressing Margaret with his longing eyes, the bells of the ancient Holy Cross Abbey began to chime. He slipped off his hood. Inwardly he struggled with whether to go and make himself known to her now. Still beautiful, her countenance was totally relaxed. She seemed so at peace.

It was a source of deep regret that when he was in her life, that was not the case. Too much emotion plagued them. Even now, after all this time, after his commitment to service and a totally new way of life, his heart told him that just to be near her again would cause turmoil. It was something neither of them needed; it was something he never wanted to do to her again.

But he knew without a doubt that he loved her deeply...even now.

The End

Printed in the United States
17191LVS00001B/258